For the Pleasure of His Company

For the Pleasure of His Company

An Affair of the Misty City

Charles Warren Stoddard

MINT EDITIONS

For the Pleasure of His Company: An Affair of the Misty City was first published in 1903.

This edition published by Mint Editions 2021.

ISBN 9781513295374 | E-ISBN 9781513295527

Published by Mint Editions®

MINT
EDITIONS

minteditionbooks.com

Publishing Director: Jennifer Newens
Design & Production: Rachel Lopez Metzger
Project Manager: Micaela Clark
Typesetting: Westchester Publishing Services

To   *   *   *   *
Who e'er she be—
That not impossible she
That shall command my heart and me.

"I returned, and saw under the sun, that the race is not to the swift, nor the battle to the strong, neither yet bread to the wise, nor yet riches to the men of understanding, nor yet favour to men of skill; but time and change happeneth to them all."

—*Ecclesiastes ix:ii*

Contents

Book Third

BOOK FIRST

Paul Clitheroe

I

What the Moon Shone on

She was a smallish moon, looking very chaste and chilly and she peered vaguely through folds of scurrying fog. She shone upon a silent street that ran up a moderate hill between far-scattered corporation gas-lamps—a street that having reached the hill top seemed to saunter leisurely across a height which had once been the most aristocratic quarter of the Misty City; the quarter was still pathetically respectable, and for three squares at least its handsome residences stared destiny in the face and stood in the midst of flower-bordered lawns, unmindful of decay. Its fountains no longer played; even its once pampered children had grown up, and the young of the present generation were of a different cast; but the street seemed not to heed these changes; indeed it was growing a little careless of itself and needed replanking. Was it a realization of this fact, I wonder, that caused it on a sudden to run violently down a steep place into the Bay, as if it were possessed of Devils? Well it might be, for the human scum of the town gathered about the base of the hill, and the nights there were unutterably iniquitous.

O that pale watcher, the Moon! She shone on a rude stairway leading up to the bare face of a cliff that topped the hill; and five and forty uncertain steps that had more than once slid down into the street below along with the wreckage of the winter rains, for the cliff was of rock and of clay and though the rock may stand until the crack of Doom, the clay mingles with the elements and an annual mud pudding, tons in weight, was deposited on the pavement of the high street, to the joy of the juveniles and the grief of the belated pedestrians. The cliff towering at the junction of the two thoroughfares shared with each its generous mud-flow and half of it descended in lavalike cascades into the depths of a ravine that crossed the high street at right angles, passing under a bridge still celebrated as a triumph of architectural ungainliness.

She shone, my Lady Moon, into that deep ravine which was half filled with shadow and made a weird picture of the place; it seemed like the bed of some dark noiseless river, the source of which was still undiscovered; and as for its mouth, no one would ever find it, or, finding, tell of it, for the few who trusted themselves to its voiceless and invisible current were heard of no more; sometimes a sharp cry for help pierced the midnight silence, and it was known upon the hill that murder was being done down yonder—that was all. Yet day by day the great tide of traffic poured through this subterranean passage, with muffled roar as of a distant sea.

She shone on all that was left of a once beautiful and imposing mansion. It crowned the very brow of the cliff; it proudly overlooked all the neighbors; it was a Gothic ruin girded about with a mantle of ivy and dense creepers, yet not all of the perennial leafage that clothed it, even to the eaves, could disguise the fact that the major portion of the mansion had been razed to the ground lest it should topple and go crashing into that gulf below. There, once upon a time, in a Gothic garden shaded by slender cypresses, walked the golden youth of the land; there, feminine lunch parties, pink teas, highly exclusive musicales and fashionable hops, flourished mightily; now the former side-door served as the front entrance to all that was left of the mansion; the stone that was rejected had become the headstone of the corner, as it were; it was an abrupt corner to be sure, with the upper half of its narrow door filled with small panes of glass; its modest threshold was somewhat worn; but upon the platform before it a large egg-shaped jar of unmistakable Chinese origin encased the roots of a flowing cactus that might have added a grace to the proudest palace in the Misty City. This was the modest portal of the Eyrie; ivy vines sheltered it like a dense thatch; ivy vines clung fast to a deep bay window that nearly filled one side of the library of the old mansion, now a living-room; ivy vines curtained the glazed wall of a conservatory where some one slept as in a bower. A weird dwelling place was this the moon shone upon, where pigeons nested and cooed at intervals in all the green nooks thereof.

She shone on the tall slim panes of glass in the bay window till they shimmered like ice, and brightened the carpet on the floor of the room—a carpet that was faded and frayed; she threw a soft glow upon the three walls beyond the window; where were low, convenient shelves of books; there were books, books, books everywhere—books of all descriptions, neither creed nor caution limited their range. Many pictures and sketches in oil or water-color—some of them unframed— were upon the walls above the bookshelves; there were bronze statuettes, graceful figures of lute-strumming troubadours upon the old-fashioned marble mantel; there were busts and medallions in plaster, and a few

CHARLES WARREN STODDARD

casts after the antique. Heaped in corners, and upon the tops of the book-shelves lay bric-a-brac in hopeless confusion; toy canoes from Kamchatka and the Southern seas; wooden masks from the burial places of the Alaskan Indians and the Theban Tombs of the Nile Kings; rude fishhooks that had been dropped in the coral seas; sharks' teeth; and the strong beak of an albatross whose webbed feet were tobacco pouches and whose hollow wing-bones were the long jointed stem of a pipe; spears and war-clubs were there, brought from the gleaming shores of reef-girdled islands; a Florentine lamp; a roll of papyrus; an idol from Easter Island, the eyes of which were two missionary shirt buttons of mother-of-pearl, of the Puritan type; your practical cannibal, having eaten his missionary, spits out the shirt buttons to be used as the eyes which see not; carved gourds were there, and calabashes; Mexican pottery; and some of the latest Pompeiian antiquities such as are miraculously discovered in the presence of the amazed and delighted tourist who secretly purchases the same for considerably more than a song.

There were pious objects, many of them resembling the Ex Votos at a shrine; an ebony and bronzed indulgenced crucifix with a history, and Sacred Hearts done in scarlet satin with flames of shining tinsel flickering from their tops.

There were vines creeping everywhere within the room, from jars that stood on brackets and made hanging gardens of themselves; creepers, yards in length, that sprung from the mouths of water-pots hidden behind objects of interest, and these framed the pictures in living green; a huge wide-mouthed vase stood in the bay window filled with a great pulu fern still nourished by its native soil—a veritable tropical island this, now basking in the moonlight far from its native clime. Japanese and Chinese lanterns were there; and an ostrich egg brought from Nubia that hung like an alabaster lamp lit by a moonbeam; and fans, of course, but quaint barbaric ones from the Orient and the Equatorial Isles; and framed and unframed photographs of celebrities each bearing an original autograph; and easy chairs, nothing but the easiest chairs from the very far-reaching one with the long arms like a pair of oars over which one throws his slippered feet, and lolls in his pajamas in memory of an East Indian season of exile, to the deep nest-like sleepy hollow quite big enough for two, in which one dozes and dreams, and out of which it is so difficult for one to rise. Over all this picturesque confusion grinned a fleshless human skull with its eye sockets and yawning jaws stuffed full of faded boutonnieres.

The moon shone, but paler now for it was growing late, on a closed coupe that rolled rapidly from the Club House in the early morning after a High Jinks night, and clattered through the streets accompanied by the matutinal milk wagons with their frequent, intermittent pauses; thus it rolled and rolled over the resounding pavement toward that house on the hill top, The Eyrie.

The vehicle zigzagged up the steep grade, and stopped at the foot of the long stairway; some one alighted and exchanged a friendly word or two with the driver, for in that lonely part of the town it was pleasant to hear the sound of one's own voice even if one was guiltily conscious of making conversation; then with a cheerful "Good-night," this some-one climbed the steps while the vehicle hurried away with its jumble of hoofs and wheels. A key was heard at the outer door; the door sagged a little in common with everything about the house—and a tenant passed into the Eyrie.

Enter Paul Clitheroe, sole scion of that melancholy house whose foundations had sunk under him, and left him, at the age of five and twenty, master of himself, but slave to fortune.

In the dim light he closed and fastened the outer door; from a hall scarcely large enough for two people to pass in, he entered the inner room with the confident step of a familiar. Having deposited hat, cane and ulster in their respective places—there was a place for everything or it would have been quite impossible to abide in that snuggery—he sank into one of the easy chairs, rolled a cigarette with meditative deliberation, lighted it and blew the smoke into the moonlight where it assumed a thousand fantastic forms.

The silence of the room seemed emphasized by the presence of its occupant; he was one who under no circumstances was likely to disturb the serenity of a house. In most cases a single room takes on the character of the one who inhabits it; this is invariably the case where the apartment is in the possession of a woman; but turn a man loose in a room, and leave him to himself for a season, and he will have made of that room a witness strong enough to condemn or condone him on the Last Day; the whole character of the place will gradually change until it has become an index to the man's nature; where this is not the case, the man is without noticeable characteristics.

Those who knew Paul Clitheroe, the solitary at the Eyrie, would at once recognize this room as his abode; those of his friends who saw this room for the first time, without knowing it to be his home, would say:

"Paul Clitheroe would fit in here." A kind of harmonious incongruity was the chief characteristic of the man and his solitary lodging.

He sat for some time as silent as the inanimate objects in that singularly silent room. An occasional turn of the wrist, the momentary flash of the ash at the end of his cigarette, the smoke-wreath floating in space—those were all that gave assurance of life; for when this solitary returned into his well-chosen solitude he seemed to shed all that was of the earth earthy, and to become a kind of spectre in a dream.

Having finished his cigarette, Paul withdrew into the conservatory, his sleeping room, half doll's house and half bower, where the ivy had crept over the top of the casement and covered his ceiling with a web of leaves. Shortly he was reposing upon his pillow, over which his holy-water font—a large crimson heart of crystal with flames of burnished gold, set upon a tablet of white marble—seemed almost to pulsate in the exquisite half-lights of approaching dawn.

It may not have been manly, or even masculine, for him thus literally to curtain his sleep, like a faun, with ivy; it may not have been orthodox for him to admit to his Valhalla some of the false Gods, and to honor them after a fashion; the one true God was duly adored, and all his saints appealed to in filial faith. That was his nature and past changing; if he could not look upon God as a Jealous God visiting His judgments with fanatical justice upon the witted and the half-witted, it was because his was a nature which had never been warped by the various social moral and religious influences brought to bear upon it.

He may have lacked judgment, in the eyes of the world, but he had never suffered seriously in consequence. It may not have been wise for him to fondly nourish tastes and tendencies that were usually quite beyond his means; but he did it, and doing it afforded him the greatest pleasure in life.

You will pardon him all this; every one did sooner or later, even those who discountenanced similar weaknesses or affectations—or whatever you are pleased to call them—in anyone else, soon found an excuse for overlooking them in his case.

He was not, thank heaven, all things to all men; all things to a few, he may have been—yea, even more than all else to some, so long as the spell lasted; to the majority, however, he was probably nothing, and less than nothing. And what of that? If he did little good in the world, he certainly did less evil; and, as he lay in his bed, under a white counterpane upon which the dawning light, sifting through the vines that curtained the glazed front of his sleeping room, fell in a mottled Japanese pattern, and while the ivy that covered the Gothic ceiling trailed long tendrils of the palest and most delicate green, each leaf glossed as if it had been varnished, this unheroic-hero, this pantheistic-devotee, this heath-enized-christian, this half-happy-go-lucky æsthetic Bohemian, lay upon his pillow, the incarnation of absolute repose.

And so the morning broke, and the early birds began to chirp in the ivy and to prune their plumage and flutter among the leaves; and down the street tramped the feet of the toilers on their way to forge and dock. Over the harbor came the daffodil light from the sun-tipped eastern hills, and it painted the waves that lapped the sleek sides of a yacht lying at anchor under the hill. A yacht that Paul had watched many a day and dreamed of many a night; for he often longed with a great longing to slip cable and hie away, even unto the utter-most parts.

II

What the Sun Shone on

He shone on the far side of the eastern azure hills and set all the tree tops in the wood beyond the wold aflame; he looked over the silhouette out of a cloudless sky upon a Bay whose breadth and beauty is one of the seven hundred wonders of the world; he paved the waves with gold, a path celestial that angels might not fear to tread. He touched the heights of the Misty City and the sea-fog that had walled it in through the night as with walls of unquarried marble—albeit the eaves had dripped in the darkness as after a summer shower—and anon the opaque vapors dissolved and fled away. There she lay, the Misty City, in all her wasted and scattered beauty; she might have been a picture for Poets to dream on and Artists to love—their wonder and their despair— but she is not; she is hideous to look upon save in the sunset or the after-glow when you cannot see her, but only the dim vision of what she might have been.

He rose as a God refreshed with sleep and called the weary to their work, and disturbed the slumbers of those that toil not and spin not, and have nothing to do but sleep.

There were no secrets from him now; every detail was discovered; and so having gilded for a moment the mossy shingles of the Eyrie he stole into the room where Paul Clitheroe passed most of his waking hours, and through the curtain of ivy and geraniums that screened the conservatory from the eyes of the curious world, and where Paul was at this moment sleeping the sleep of the just. From the bed of the ravine below the Eyrie rose the rumble and roar of traffic. The hours passed by. The sleeper began to turn uneasily on his pillow. The sound of hurrying feet was heard upon the board walks in front of the Eyrie-cliff; many voices, youthful voices, swelled the chorus that told of the regiments of children now hastening to school. From dreamland Paul returned by easy stages to the work-a-day world. He arose donned a trailing garment with angel sleeves and a large crucifix embroidered in scarlet upon the breast—that robe made of him a cross between a Monk and a Marchioness—slipped his feet into sandals and entered the larger chamber which was at once living-room and library. He opened the shutters in the deep bay window and greeted the day with the silent solemnity of a fire-worshipper; gave drink to his potted palms and ferns and flowering plants; let his eye wander leisurely over the titles of his books; lingered a little while over his favorites and patted some of them fondly on the back. Taking a small key from its nail by the door he opened the mail box without, carrying his letters to his writing table and leaving them there unopened. He loved to speculate as to whom the writers were and what they may have said to him. This piqued his curiosity, and tided him over a scant breakfast at an inexpensive but fly-blown restaurant where he was wont to eat or make a more or less brave effort to eat whenever he had the wherewithal to settle for the same. Breakfast over and gone the young man returned to his Eyrie, and in due course was at his writing table, and at work upon the weekly article that had been appearing in the Sunday issue of one of the popular Dailies for an indefinite period, and the price of which had on several occasions kept him from becoming a conspicuous object of charity.

Having written himself out for the day, as he was apt to in a few hours, he wandered down to the Club for a bit of refreshment which was sure to be forthcoming, for his friends there were ever ready to dine him, or more frequently to wine him, merely for the pleasure of his company.

So the afternoon waned and the dinner hour approached; fortunately this hour was usually bespoken and for a little while at least he was lapped in luxury. On his way home he was very apt to turn in at the wicker gates of a typical German Rathskellar where he was unmolested; where the blustering pipes of a colossal orchestrion brayed through an aria from Trovatore with more sound than sentiment and all unmindful of modulation.

He was at home by midnight, for the beer and the bravura ceased to flow at the witching hour. Then he lounged in the easy chair, gradually and not unconsciously shedding all the worldly influences that had been clothing him as with a hair-shirt even since he first went forth that morning. Safely he sank into the silence of the place. Every breath he drew was balm; every moment healing. So he passed into the silence, enfolded by invisible arms that led him gently to his pillow where he sank to sleep with the trustful resignation of a tired babe.

If this routine was ever varied it was a variation with a vengeance. "From grave to gay, from lively to severe" might have been engraved upon his escutcheon. It chanced that the family motto was Festina

CHARLES WARREN STODDARD

Lente; this also was appropriate; had he not all his life made haste slowly? For this very reason he had been accounted one of the laziest of his kind; his indolence was a byword merely because he did not throw himself into an easy chair at the Club, of an evening, and bewail his fate; because he did not puff and blow and talk often of the work he had accomplished, was accomplishing, or hastening forward to accomplishment. With all his faults, thank heaven, that sin cannot be charged against him.

III

Scribes and Pharisees

The Hotel de France stood on the edge of an Arcadian settlement, some few miles from the Misty City. At the time of which I write this Arcadia was a wide-spreading grove of oaks among which a few modest houses were scattered; cow-paths meandered over sand and sod; flocks and herds fed peacefully under the shade, where in the gloaming, the cry of the cow-herd and the clang of the contralto bells that hung to the throats of the milch-kine, made musical the close of day.

This lovely, if somewhat lonely land, was usually referred to as "Over the Bay." The ferry was an hour and a half in reaching it, when the tide was high; at low tide the ferry sometimes lay motionless on the bar just beyond the mud-flats for one, two or even three hours; that is until the tide turned, and set her free again. It was a Sabbath day's journey, and one that was oftener taken on that day than any other. Only the rustics and those whose business affairs were not too exacting could afford to dwell in Arcadia.

The Hotel de France would not have looked out of place in any Mexican town. It stood directly upon an unpaved street; it was long, and rather low, and severely plain of face: it had two stories with doors and windows of the self-same pattern—they were divided down the middle from floor to ceiling. A long narrow gallery resting upon slender iron brackets, ran the length of the building at the base of the second story. One might expect to see there at any moment Senoritas in loose flowing gowns, with guitars and fans and cigarettes, and to hear low musical dialogue and the tinkling accompaniment of the instrument one embraces; not infrequently this was possible, but oftener the vivacious Frenchman made the house ring with his loquacity, while at times the solid, not to say sodden good fellowship of the German was attested in the clang of the high-lifted glass.

In the rear of the hotel a long and narrow garden ran down to the water's edge; a tide-washed estuary separated the garden from a broad marsh; beyond the marsh a grove of wind-warped oaks marked the middle distance and compared well with the purple outlines of the distant foot-hills of the Coast Range. A long, one-story wooden building with a veranda, sheltered the windy side of the garden. It was divided into single rooms, with a door and a window in each; arbors with tables of various sizes in them, were scattered over the grounds; there were several spaces allotted to the out-of-door games so popular with those who habitually dine *al fresco,* and everywhere the garden paths were hedged with artichokes that strove in vain to hide a hopeless but happy mingling of flowers and kitchen vegetables.

In one of these arbors sat a little group of Scribes and Pharisees; the burden of the day was over; for a few weeks past this merry company had met each evening and prolonged their dinner until the hour of retiring. This was Liberty Hall, and as is often the case, the fact being perfectly patent on the face of it, there was less conspicuous unpleasantness than one sometimes encounters in professedly ultra-respectable establishments. The Pharisees were not all Scribes.

Said Archer, the chief scribe, whose word was law, and therefore for the most part smiled at—"I hear young Clitheroe has fallen foul of a highly accomplished young person who has been bred abroad."

"O, yes! Of course! With him the latest is always the likeliest and the loveliest. You should have seen him in the wake of that Russian quasi-Princess, at the Pavilion during the late Exposition. She fairly swamped him with her effusiveness."

It was Twitter who spoke; Twitter of one of the minor dailies in the Misty City, whose two columns of Sunday scintillations were a starred feature in that journal. Twitter was considered one of the bright and shining lights of the wild-western journalism.

"Now that is hardly fair," broke in a very admirable lady known among her friends as the Pompadour; "Paul met the Russian abroad; she is not a princess, and never pretended to be one. She and Paul are warm friends and old ones. If she was effusive, it was probably her nature to be so, and Paul is not in the least to blame for it."

Twitter, who was quite a dapper little figure, turned to the Pompadour—"What is it that you women see in Paul to attract you? Women are always making an ass of him."

"There is a singular charm in youth," replied the Pompadour, "it is fragrant, it is ephemeral, it is very precious in the eyes of those who have grown a little world-weary."

"Like Madam," chimed in Archer, whose admiration for the lady was no secret. She continued without noticing the interruption:

"The fact that Paul is not utterly spoiled proves that he is worthy of the esteem he has won; most boys would have been ruined by half the flattery he has received."

"Flattery?" queried Archer; "Flattery? What is flattery? Paul Clitheroe has been held in the laps of the ladies ever since he was a baby; they have fondled him as freely as if he were a girl. You may have observed, Madam, that he puts up his mouth to be kissed when he meets a woman, just as naturally as any babe or suckling."

"Paul is nothing but a boy—you ought to be ashamed to speak of him in this manner." The Pompadour was magnificent in her half-affected indignation.

"Yes," replied Archer, "and these are the very boys that set at defiance all the usages of Society and presume upon the favor of every one they are brought in contact with." Archer was a little nettled, and yet he was fond of Paul, and often spoke in his defence. Then Twitter twittered:

"When Paul Clitheroe is lonesome, he goes forth; he is at once gobbled up by some one in search of a literary lion, and she fondles him so long as he finds it amusing. When he wearies—even so soon as he begins to fear that he may presently weary, he departs. I've seen the fellow sit in the most passive manner, while his lady admirers fondly caressed him. I've heard one of these silly women say, 'I never see Paul Clitheroe but I feel the inclination to take him in my arms and kiss him.' Pah, this sort of thing sickens me!"

"Well—she might have kissed him with perfect impunity," responded the Pompadour, "he'd have taken it as complacently as a statue."

At this moment a gentleman approached the party. Then Archer spoke: "Mme. la Pompadour, permit me to present Foxlair of Foxlair."

The Pompadour was superb as she graciously acknowledged the introduction; the powdered hair and the patch could have added nothing to her regal beauty.

Foxlair was a son of the South; a man of mystery; all kinds of romantic rumors were current concerning him,—that he had been a Rebel Spy, or the husband of a Rebel Spy, and a privateersman in the Spanish Main, etc., etc. Of all these he could speak most entertainingly; giving much elaborate and picturesque detail, when encouraged by a circle of appreciative listeners. Foxlair was swarthily handsome, with the physique of a trained athlete.

Conversation became general; certain extras, after-dinner delicacies, were suggested and discussed. Diogenes came late—dear, delightful,

Diogenes, whose youth seemed to have spontaneously matured and whose gravity was of the light comedy cast. While Archer edited one newspaper and wrote for several others, Diogenes also sat in an editorial chair. This very evening it was proposed that Foxlair should found a paper at once and assume editorial management. To tell the whole truth this is exactly what he did. Arcadia had but two political organs. Important elections were approaching; Foxlair made it evident to a third political party that an organ devoted to the airing of the principles of this party—such as they were—was absolutely necessary; the week following he issued the initial number of a new weekly, and there was great rejoicing among the artichokes at the Hotel de France.

When the company was merriest, who should enter but Paul Clitheroe. He had been spending some days with new-found friends at Santa Rosa; they had all come to a most perfect understanding and an alluring future had been blocked out for him; but of this he proposed to say nothing for the present. That was another secret—he seemed at last to be growing secretive; he was again saying to himself as he had once said to some one else, "little secrets are cozy." Perhaps he had just begun to realize that this is ever the case, and that the one who has a secret to keep has a treasure, and the possession of it seems somehow to give him an immense advantage over his fellowmen.

When Paul made his appearance he was greeted with acclaim. This did not in the least disconcert him; there is no doubt about it, he was immensely popular, and even those who did not admire him, or approve of his manners and customs, or were perhaps envious of him, yet treated him kindly, if not cordially. He was hailed by all present; he went at once to salute the Pompadour, and in the most natural and unaffected manner kissed her upon the forehead; she embraced him in a half-maternal fashion, and, without embarrassment, called for another glass and filling it with the wine of the country, pressed it upon the young man. He was acquainted with all present save the stranger-guest of the evening, Foxlair, and they were presently brought together, and at once entered into an animated conversation.

There are some people who invariably make a favorable first impression. They may or they may not sustain themselves; they may even grow in grace from day to day; Paul was one of these. He had, at times taken a new acquaintance by storm; he had, on occasions, been thrown together with strangers at some way-station, when for a few hours they were in one another's company, and these chance acquaintances had never forgotten him; he had made no effort to be entertaining; he had merely been perfectly natural. New faces or new forms of speech had always interested him, for a while at least; they seemed to quicken his wits, and the interest he felt in them was genuine, for the time being; perhaps it was as much curiosity as interest, for he was fond of studying people, and having formed an impression of a person he met for the first time—probably it was intuition—he liked very much to test these subjects and see how near he had come to the truth. Sometimes, when he had formed an unfavorable opinion of one whom he knew but slightly, his conscience smote him and he resolved to pay no heed to his first impression, but to do the unconscious victim of his judgment full justice. In such a case the two would become more or less friendly and familiar but invariably, sooner or later, he found good cause for quietly withdrawing, if not actually shunning the acquaintance; he had now proof positive that his first impression was correct. Genuine intuitions are infallible.

Foxlair, being a thoroughbred Southerner, was fond of horse-flesh; the night was a particularly fine one, with perfect moonlight; Foxlair proposed a drive. In Bohemia everything and anything is in season. A drive was at once decided upon, and shortly after from the adjoining livery came a conveyance large enough to accommodate all those of the party who cared to participate. Foxlair on the box, with a spirited span in hand, proved himself an admirable whip. The country roads—they could hardly be called turn-pikes—for miles around were threaded by the somewhat boisterous company. Many a silent farmhouse, where the inmates had no doubt long been wrapped in slumber, was startled by an impromptu chorus of war-whoops; dim lights appeared in remote mansions where the startled sleepers arose to peer from windows upon the landscape, white under the cloudless moon, and they saw in the distance a flying shadow with a veil of dust trailing like a smoke-wraith in its wake, and heard cries that fluttered the barn-fowls until the cock's shrill crow was hurled after them defiantly.

Did this delight the soul of Paul Clitheroe? He could not have told you himself. The midnight drive was not without certain picturesque features; the wide silent landscape; the infinite peace that brooded over it; the profound mystery that stands guard at the threshold of the house of sleep—Paul was forever wondering who they were that were within, and beyond which of all the windows lay the fairest sleeper; and what dreams might at that moment be visiting her pillow; and yonder where a brighter light was blazing—it was hardly a student that was burning the midnight oil in such a quarter—were they ill there?—a watcher by the bed of pain would scarcely burn so bright a light; sleep had forsaken the chamber and Paul wondered why. Even when the shouts were the wildest and the horses were careering madly over roads that were more accustomed to the spreading hoof of the ox than the sharp stroke of the iron shoe, he was lost in curious dreams and reveries. The various currents of air through which they passed, the warmer like a breath of the south, the cooler with a touch of the autumn in them, were full of suggestion and seemed to shape his dreams. Not one in that merry company knew his mood; they thought him unusually silent, that was all; and as he was considered a creature of moods, his silence was not questioned.

So they returned to the Hotel de France, which was apparently deserted, and as the beauty of the night was quite irresistible, they repaired to the foot of the garden and sat upon the benches by the shore. Archer was noticeably exhilarated; he apostrophized the moon, and the ebon water at their feet where the moon's fair image was wreathed with fiery serpents, like a head of Medusa done in gold; he quoted the poets with admirable effect, and talked when interested with the fine culture of a scholar, the appreciation of a poet, and the art of a trained elocutionist. His was a most attractive personality. Paul was fond of this clever and many-sided litterateur; he often sought the society of the men who seemed to care little for the companionship of any one save the Pompadour; Archer had been the first to note and call attention to the budding poetic talent of young Clitheroe. It was the fate of this youth to begin his career in a provincial community, which was to a certain extent isolated from the world. Journalism was rampant; it fed upon the virgin fatness of the land; writers of marked genius were developing, somewhat prematurely, perhaps; strength and crudity went hand in hand; they were the foster-children of originality. Paul Clitheroe was the youngest of the writers who had begun to attract attention in the local journals and magazines. He was lauded by the editors who graciously, and for a long period, printed his effusions gratuitously.

They printed them with more impartiality than justice; he wrote with a prolific pen, sent everything to press, and was almost never "declined with thanks." Of course his verses were of varying degrees of merit; none of them were very good—or would today be likely to attract attention outside of his immediate circle of friends; but in the Misty City, and in all the provincial towns that hoped some day to rival if not distance the Metropolis in literary culture and in everything else, the poetical efforts of Paul Clitheroe were often a subject of discussion. So it came to pass that the rival editors who, half in jest and half in earnest were ready to cross pens in bloodless combat, found it a pleasant thing to gibbet the Clitheroe bantlings that were being rushed upon the market with such unseemly haste. If Archer were in the mood to hail Clitheroe as the rising star of song, he did so in a manner that was calculated to impress the unprejudiced reader with profound respect for the poetaster. Thereupon the quasi-critics scattered throughout the land pounced upon the inoffensive Paul, and rent him limb from limb; it was not for any lack of appreciation on the part of the disaffected critics that Paul's verses were measured and found wanting; these very editors and critics would have published the self-same productions and probably with some complimentary editorial accompaniment; but here was a convenient opportunity publicly to question the critical acumen of Archer, for example, and they hastened to embrace it. Paul's feelings were never for a moment taken into consideration. It is just as well that they were not; he was early learning a lesson that all writers, and especially all poets, must sooner or later learn. He was learning that the judgment of one mind alone must never be taken for more than the judgment of one mind alone; that is all it ever under any circumstances can be; the judgment of a mind that may not be in sympathy with the writer whose work is being weighed in the balance: moreover the critic too often dips his pen in bile. The judgment of two minds is not much worth considering—nor the judgment of two dozen. Time alone can establish the worth of literary work. Paul Clitheroe discovered this gospel truth when he was yet a boy. The conviction was early forced upon him; and though his feelings were often wounded by the scornful or cruel truths from pens editorial, he was growing in wisdom, and the fulsome flattery which was wont to salve his wounds, while it may have soothed him, did not harden him, or teach him to overestimate his worth.

Certainly when Archer, in the most influential literary weekly published at that time, the pride of the coast, lauded Paul's first-born volume of verses to the skies, and then, a few days later through the columns of another journal to which at intervals he contributed anonymously, attacked himself and flayed the young poet alive, Paul knowing Archer to be the author of both articles was somewhat shocked. Perhaps for a few days following his discovery his faith in humanity was shaken. Twitter who had on this very night embraced Paul as he joined the dinner party in the arbor, wrote stinging paragraphs about him; burlesqued certain of his weaknesses and mannerisms and ridiculed him, sometimes within his hearing. Paul was at first inclined to fly the whole crew and bury himself in some convenient obscurity. He did fly from the world at intervals; the temptation to do so was irresistible, no matter what the provocation may have been. This is why he had nested himself in comparative seclusion at the ivy-mantled Eyrie. But his heart was full of longing; he craved sympathy and love; he gave both freely—far too freely, as he discovered on a certain few occasions. They were sometimes ill bestowed as he was often, no doubt, misunderstood; but he had never outgrown a certain childlike ingenuousness and he was not likely to outgrow it. Later on, experience and worldly wisdom came to his rescue when he was most in danger and withheld him when he was on the point of sacrificing himself; and he was getting on very nicely with the world, the flesh and the devil; and not one of these three disturbed him to any great extent, and not one of them ever did him a lasting injury.

To prove that he was still himself, trusting, ingenuous, impulsive, that very morning—it was morning before the party broke up by the shore at the foot of the garden—when Foxlair was about to return to his lodgings he invited Paul to accompany him and, without a moment's hesitation, the lad did so, and for a week following they were inseparable.

IV

Foxlair the Faithless

For one week Paul Clitheroe was the constant companion of his latest friend. Foxlair, who was playing the host in mezzo Monte Cristo fashion, gave him a desk-seat in the editorial room of the new journal; beguiled him with numberless tales of personal adventure; dined him, wined him, took him for drives among the foot hills, through the wild, warm, spicy canyons, where the birds, and the blossoms, and the bees, refreshed the senses of the sensuous young poet. Foxlair was fond of boating, and pulled a tireless oar; many an hour with Paul was passed among the tules, the friends finding much to enjoy in common, and Foxlair in his big, brotherly fashion making of Paul's life a happy holiday.

Paul's friends had ceased to wonder at him; they had for the most part ceased to reason with him; he was adjudged incorrigible, incurable, in brief over-impressible. If upon the shortest notice he could take up with a mysterious personage—not always was one as attractive as this Southerner; could drop his old friends without "giving notice;" neglect his engagements; leave his Eyrie unvisited for an indefinite period, and replenish his wardrobe whenever and wherever he found it most convenient: if he could not employ the talent God had given him in an honest and straightforward manner, preferring rather to contribute gratuitously as much prose and verse as Foxlair had need of to fill his columns; if he were content to live without a motive in life, playing the butterfly to his heart's content and letting the world go by as if it were of no moment—there was nothing to do but to wash one's hands of him and shrug one's shoulders, and leave him to his fate.

Foxlair was possessed of strong personal magnetism; there was no manner of doubt about that. He easily and speedily won the interest if not the confidence of those with whom he was brought in contact. This was especially the case with ladies, and more particularly the ladies of the South.

They feted him; they made a star feature of him on all social occasions; through Paul he had met a few of them, and those few had hastened to extend the circle of his acquaintants. While Paul was still his intimate, it was whispered among his male associates that Foxlair was more or less of a fiction; that his personal history was not reliable; that he could, when necessary, supply facts in a case where facts were sorely needed to make whole the thread of his narrative.

He carried about with him in a neat morocco case the photograph of a lovely child; he had on various occasions, when being entertained by the highly respectable mothers of highly respectable families, drawn this portrait from his bosom and dropped the conventional tear of paternal affection over it, "My daughter," it was his custom to say to his hostess; and such friends as may have been present, shared his emotions. If there was a question as to the identity of his wife, and the validity, yea, even probability of his marriage—and there was such a question, which to this day remains unanswered—it worried him not. But there was a surprise in store for those who had been witnesses of his paternal sensibility. Paul had never seen this photograph, but a lady friend to whom Paul had presented Foxlair in the first flush of their friendship, meeting him one day inquired for news of him.

"He has not called on me for an age," said the lady, "he has not even paid his dinner-call; and stranger than all, I showed him, at this dinner, a photograph of my little daughter which he admired extravagantly. That photograph has disappeared."

Paul was perplexed. "Have you not seen the picture since his last visit?" he asked.

"No; and I have searched high and low; when did you last see your friend?"

"Two or three days ago. He was in the city and made the Eyrie his headquarters."

"Where is he now?"

"That I cannot say, nor do I know when I shall see him again. His journal was not a success, and its publication has been discontinued. What he is doing now, what his plans are, and where he is likely to go next, is more than I can conjecture;" and Paul made a movement as if to take his leave.

The lady still detained him. She continued, with a slight hardness in her voice, "When you next see your friend, will you kindly ask him to return the photograph of my daughter? I don't care to have the picture in his possession;" and bowing a little stiffly, she went her way.

Paul's cheek was burning; his heart was beating with uncomfortable rapidity; he found himself wandering aimlessly along the street, striving to repress his rising indignation. Noticing that he was not far from the Eyrie, and being anxious to avoid seeing any one at that moment he turned his steps homeward.

How sweet the dear old chambers seemed to him then; how very, very quiet it was there; how peaceful, how restful! The sun streamed in through the big Gothic bay window; the ferns and flowers in the room filled the air with delicious fragrance. All his books so neatly arranged, standing shoulder to shoulder and just of a height; his pretty bric-a-brac suggesting a thousand souvenirs of the past, of his life in the Islands, where he fancied he was happiest. O, why did he ever care to leave the place? Why was he not satisfied to bury himself among those beloved objects, and hold no further intercourse with the world—save by letter? Ah, yes, by letter! He arose, took the key from its tack on the side of the book shelves nearest the door and opened his letter-box to find letters within. He examined the superscriptions and recognized the handwriting. A letter from Archer, a letter from Twitter, and one from Diogenes. What did it mean? It was not often that he heard from so many at once, at least in that quarter. He concluded to let the letters lie unopened until after his siesta; they might contain ill news; he must fortify himself with wholesome and refreshing sleep, for the world was getting the better of him.

Never had the conservatory looked more bowerlike than now; the loveliest green twilight pervaded it; the soft arms of sleep seemed to fold him about as he entered the bower and lead him gently to his pillow. In a few moments he had forgotten and forgiven everything.

He was presently awakened by a nervous tap at his outer door; it irritated him. He lay upon his bed, wishing the intruder would depart in peace. The knock was impatiently repeated; Paul arose, but before he could make himself presentable and reach the door, a cane was drawn swiftly and almost viciously across the inside shutters—the window being raised made this practicable; he was called sharply by name and he at once recognized the voice of the speaker. He opened the door to Foxlair, who entered somewhat surlily. His face was scarlet; he did not seem himself; Paul had never before known him in such a strait. Throwing himself heavily into the oriental chair he stretched his legs upon the long paddle-like arms and tapped his boot toes, first one and then the other with his cane; it was Paul's cane; a souvenir he prized highly—a handsomely turned stick of some precious wood brought from a far country and which he held too sacred to be worn by anybody. Puffing out his cheeks, and mouthing for a moment, Foxlair spoke:

"Why didn't you open to me? I knew well enough that you were in. There was the key in the keyhole."

"I was sleeping," said Paul meekly. "I was on my way to the door, when you struck the blind." There was an awkward silence. Foxlair's arm was thrown over his head, his hand rested upon the back of the chair; his eyes gradually closed and he was presently breathing heavily. Paul dropped into a reverie that caused him to knit his brow. Waking suddenly out of it, he went over to his writing table, took the letters from it and opened them one after another; they ran as follows:

Dear Clitheroe:

What has become of our quondam friend, the faithless Foxlair? He has quit Arcadia in a very unceremonious manner, leaving debts on every hand. If you know anything of his whereabouts there are many here who would be glad to be informed of it. When are you coming over again? We miss you.

Fraternally,
Archer

"P.S.: The Pompadour will add a line."

My Dearest Paul:

I hope nothing serious has happened to Foxlair. He has mysteriously disappeared and we hear very unpleasant reports concerning him. I trust he hasn't wronged you in any way.

"Do come to us soon; I have so much to say to you—and I've a great secret to divulge.

Ever most affectionately,
P.

Next came the following:

Amiable Idiot:

Your henchman, Foxlair—or are you his?—has vanished like the sweet south o'er a bank of violets, 'stealing and giving odour'; to tell the truth the odour is anything but pleasant in the nostrils of his acquaintances. If you know aught of his whereabouts, the constable of Arcadia will, no doubt, be glad to hear from you, though as yet I have heard of no proffered reward and you are therefore possibly beyond the reach of temptation.

"Really now, isn't it about time you were beginning to reform? We shall be charmed to aid you in so laudable an effort.

"In a Bohemian sense,

Yours to command,
Twitter

There was yet one other message, unread. Foxlair was moving in his chair; his sleep was evidently anything but restful.

Paul opened the last envelope and read:

"If Foxlair is within your reach I'd advise you to recommend him quitting these parts as early as convenient. I hear the sheriff is on his track.

Yours,
Diogenes

While these letters were still in Paul's lap, and he filled with amazement and alarm, Foxlair awoke. He seemed less disturbed than when he entered the Eyrie an hour before. What to say to the accused and how to say it was soon the question which puzzled Paul. While he was shocked almost beyond expression by the startling revelations concerning the conduct of his friend, and for a few moments was seized with indignation, and upon the point of giving expression to charges and denunciations which he would certainly have regretted later, he resolved to control his emotion as best he could. Foxlair yawned audibly, shook his head somewhat snappishly, as if to free himself from drowsiness, rubbed his eye and arose to kick down the hem of his trousers. Paul said:

"So you have left Arcadia for good?"

"Have I? Who says I have?"

"That is the current report."

"On this point," muttered Foxlair, growing nettled, "perhaps I am the best authority."

"Certainly you should be; but where a rumor is widespread and generally credited there must be some occasion for it."

CHARLES WARREN STODDARD

"I don't know what you are referring to, and it matters nothing to me what may be said or thought concerning my actions or my motives. I am a gentleman and a free-lance; I hold myself accountable to no man that lives!" Here he straightened himself up to his full height, and seemed to grow at least two inches taller.

"Nor woman either?" queried Paul.

Foxlair turned suddenly, where he stood, and with a vicious glance cried sharply:

"What do you mean?"

"I mean," rejoined Paul, who could hardly keep his voice from quivering—"I mean that the lady to whom I introduced you, and from whom you borrowed a certain photograph, the likeness of her child, begs that I will procure the same from you and return it to her."

Foxlair grew pale, compressed his lips, was silent for a moment, and then taking the photograph in its morocco case from an inner pocket of his coat, tossed it with a contemptuous gesture upon the table.

Paul sat motionless; he was beginning to tremble all over; this he invariably did when laboring under excitement of any kind and it always vexed him when he realized how little control he had over himself. Presently Foxlair, having regained his self-control, took up the photograph and placed it in Paul's hand, saying as he did so, "I beg your pardon, dear boy, I ought to have returned that picture long ago."

He touched Paul lightly on the shoulder in friendly recognition, rolled a cigarette in a very elegant and leisurely manner, and having lighted it, he resumed:

"As for Arcadia, it's a dull place and I'm heartily sick of it. I'm again beginning to thirst for adventure; I must go somewhere in search of change. I always get stagnant after stopping a while in a place; I shall rot if I stop longer in this latitude." He paused for breath, and began pacing up and down the room with a swinging stride—one who didn't admire him would call it a strut.

"Yes, I quite agree with you," Paul rejoined, in a natural voice and a spirit much quieted, "one must have an occasional change of scene, that is if there are figures in one's landscape. As for Nature, she is changeable enough; the only objection to the desert island is that it is usually tropical and its summer is perpetual. It's the handsomest and most gorgeously decorative summer that ever was; but it is so beautiful in the beginning that it can never be more beautiful, or less beautiful, and mere beauty, sensuous summer beauty, becomes a burden after a while. If one is a solitary, on the other hand, one weans himself from everybody and everything—at least, he is supposed to—and thus expecting nothing, he misses nothing if nothing comes to him. We lose interest in faces; fellows talk themselves out and so need a change of human temperament, and taste, and talent, once in a while. I know well enough that I do!"

"Look here, Paul Clitheroe," cried Foxlair, turning suddenly upon the youth who was seated in his deep, sleepy-hollow chair, "I love you better than any fellow I ever met. You understand me; these brutes about us are incapable of it." He came and sat on the arm of Paul's chair, facing him, his two hands resting on Paul's shoulders, and resumed: "Let's leave this cursed land. Let us sail into the South Seas. You love them and so do I. There we can be princes, or even kings, and have retinues of lovely slaves, and live a life,—oh, such a life as here we can only dream of. Come, will you go to Tahiti, Samoa, Tongatabu?"

"How shall we get there? My faith is not sufficient to float my feet upon the face of the waters; I cannot ship before the mast—and I haven't a cent in the world!" said Paul.

"I haven't a cent in the world either, and for the most part I don't need one. I believe the world owes me a living, it has paid up to date;" after a thoughtful pause; "why can't we go as traveling correspondents, you for one paper and I for another? If we can't get money in advance to pay our way in the cabin, I'll go before the mast. I can do it—have done it before. Once on the other side of the sea we are all right, no one can touch us there!"

"Who wants to touch us here?" asked Paul, in affected surprise.

"Oh, nobody." This was said so carelessly Paul began to doubt that his friend had done anything out of the way. He was beginning to feel the subtle charm that a sensitive nature so easily and so freely responds to. Paul might indeed, had it been possible, suddenly and impulsively have departed for the Antipodes with Foxlair; but the impossibility—evident to him, though Foxlair affected to ignore it—the impossibility was no very great disappointment and the proposition was entertained for a few moments only.

Paul looked at his watch; it was now the hour of an appointment he was especially anxious to keep. He could not invite Foxlair to accompany him. He was still suspicious, and feared further revelations of a damaging nature. He wondered why he was not more angry with his friend; why he had not made a clean breast of the whole matter, and demanded an explanation—no doubt he had some right to. In one sense he was a coward; in another he was not. He tried to justify his own silence by arguing that he had as yet heard only one side of the case; that until he had fully informed himself he had no sufficient cause for accusing Foxlair of deliberate dishonesty. He would wait a day and make further inquiry; meanwhile he would shelter the fugitive—if, indeed, he was a fugitive—and no one would be any the wiser. In thus doing he felt that he was doing no more than any one friend should do for another. He would still champion the poor fellow's cause.

Foxlair recalled an engagement for an hour somewhat later in the evening; meanwhile he was to rest at the Eyrie—putting the key beneath the doormat on the steps when he departed. He would spend the night with Paul. Whoever returned first should admit the other; the lighted lamp within would notify the last comer that he was to knock for admittance. Foxlair was never more hearty and affectionate, and Paul was resolved to stand by him to the last and to listen to no further attacks upon his character.

Late that evening, finding himself near the Concordia Beer Hall and hearing the bray of the colossal orchestrion, Paul entered. It was long since he had visited the place. The old, friendly proprietor had departed; with him most of the familiar faces had disappeared. It was well; Paul could sit for a while and collect his scattered thoughts. His beer was ordered. He sat alone musing at a table in a somewhat obscure corner of the large hall. He was smoking and ruminating, and for a time took no particular notice of his neighbors. Presently his eye fell upon a figure he seemed to recognize. It was familiar, and yet it was not familiar. The form was that of one person, and the chief outer garment was that of another. Paul grew more perplexed the longer he strove to explain this mystery. It was as if his astral body, clothed even as in flesh, had adjourned to an adjacent table, and there seated itself with its back to him. It sat at a long table in the center of the room where there was a scattered collection of journals in all languages, enough to suit the several tastes of a cosmopolitan patronage. It had for a time been casting about among these papers in an aimless fashion, as if merely to kill time; it had ordered a glass of beer and turned again to the literature of the world. Suddenly it had found something that interested it; it snatched a paper eagerly, read the head-lines of a certain conspicuously featured article, and showed no little agitation in the reading thereof. Paul, now thoroughly interested, looked more closely at the mysterious figure;

there was no mistake about it—that mackintosh was the counterpart of one he brought with him from England, and the like of which had, until this hour, been unknown upon the Coast. The mackintosh was the mackintosh of Paul Clitheroe, but the face—it turned in a favorable light just at that moment—the face was the face of Foxlair. He had finished reading the article; he had rushed through it in evident excitement, and, crushing the paper in his fists, he dashed it upon the floor, seized his cane—Paul's precious souvenir—and stepped quickly from the hall: his beer was left untouched, so hasty had been his exit.

Paul picked up the paper from the floor where it had been thrown and smoothed it out. There, in all its glaring type was an article, heavily headed, the reading of which nearly took his breath away. It was unmistakably the work of Twitter, and Twitter had not failed to drag Paul's name into the story of the exploits of Foxlair. He read: The Prince of Frauds at last exposed. An Arrant Knave betrays the confidence of friends. A deep, designing villain in the guise of a gentleman is finally unmasked, etc., etc.

The article was already the subject of animated discussion at the Club, where Paul had introduced Foxlair, and where Foxlair had plied a guest-ticket daily, yea, almost hourly, so long as it was available. There was now, it seems, a considerable amount of money due the Club for the consumption of unpaid-for wines, liquors and cigars, as well as various sums unsettled among certain clubmen in the line of debts of honor. It was not a pleasing predicament for Paul to find himself in, and the shock was a sharp one; yet having his own name coupled with that of the now notorious Foxlair was the least of his troubles.

Paul was too used to newspaper notoriety to allow this somewhat sensational episode to seriously disturb him. The vision of that face did perplex him, and perplexed him mightily. He at once repaired to the Eyrie; would he find Foxlair within, with a satisfactory explanation or denial? No, there was no light burning when he climbed the rickety stairs. He found the key under the door-mat and nervously entered his chambers. He lighted a light and made a search of the apartment. To begin with, the mackintosh was gone; the precious cane was gone with it; his favorite scarf-pin likewise; and a ring he dearly prized but seldom wore, it being loose on his finger and he fearing he might some day lose it. Trousers? Yes, the dress trousers and vest which Foxlair had worn on two occasions, when he was addressing fashionable audiences; a difference in the modeling of the two young men perhaps, saved Paul his coat. Anything else? Much else missing, no doubt to be discovered later on.

That night Paul slept a sleep broken again and again by imaginary knockings upon the door or window. He still believed that Foxlair had not heartlessly betrayed him, and that he would anon return and make all square.

Foxlair was never again seen of men in those parts; he was never heard of, save indirectly. He had proved himself utterly unworthy of the confidence and respect of any one, and yet Paul was always trying to condone his errors, and always hoping that some day his friend would vindicate himself, and therefore he could not conscientiously upbraid the unhappy outcast, or think of him without the tenderest regret.

V

Owing to Circumstances

"IfI could only stop right here, and not see anybody—except somebody once in a while, when I wished to, and that somebody just the right one to see!"

Paul Clitheroe stood in the bay window of the Eyrie looking over the roofs upon the shining waters of the sky. He had given drink to his flowering plants; they were all flourishing. During his frequent and sometimes protracted absences his landlady—he thought her an ideal— kept his apartment in perfect order. She was proud of it and proud of him, even when he didn't pay his rent promptly. She had said to him once upon a time, when she found him unusually depressed and she suspected the occasion of his dejection, "Don't worry about the rent, Mr. Clitheroe; I am in no hurry for it; I can easily wait your time; I assure you it doesn't inconvenience me at all."

That was consoling; Clitheroe could hardly resist a temptation to make a will in her favor; he wanted her to help herself to anything in his rooms and to always feel at liberty to do so.

"If I could only stop right here," he echoed, with a sigh, hanging his pea-green toy watering-pot on its particular nail in the corner of the window where it instantly assumed a bric-a-brackish air that well became it; "If I could only stop right here, I could go to work this minute and make a living, and be ever so happy and contented. Why won't people leave me alone? Why need I be beckoned, called, forced out into the world, where I find a thousand distractions and where, after all, I have never really felt at my ease? If I could only sit down here and write—write the kind of things I wish to write—O, I would take such pleasure in it, and I am sure, in this way, I should do my best work!"

He had often been advised to write his autobiography. He had even tried to block out a series of chapters and books; of course there must be books; *Book First—Babyhood.* A little book of nurses' tales; he could not be expected to remember much about that. *Book Second—Childhood.* Therein he would preach a lesson to those parents and guardians who treat children as if they were little fools—he would dedicate that book to them—in most cases children very early discover their elders to be the bigger fools. *Book Third—Boyhood.* That would be a long book, full of growing pains, both of the body and the soul. He seemed to recall the geography of every inch of Book Third. *Book Fourth—Youth.* Full of aspirations and desires and dreams. *Book Fifth*—Manhood. Serious and speculative. And so on; and so on: the trouble would be how to keep within bounds: such a work might go on forever; every year might add its volume; for some men are born to an endless round of experiences; on the slightest investments they reap enormous profits.

Clitheroe had sometimes thought of another work he would like to write. More than once, yea, half a score of times, he had been taken in hand by his lady friends, one after another, and each in her turn had striven earnestly and determinedly to mould the young man: for the time he had become as clay in the hands of the potter. He was probably allured at first; more or less charmed for the season; and then found himself entangled and ill at ease; it was seldom that he had been enabled to extricate himself from these entanglements without considerable derangement of the social atmosphere; those experiences, no two of them alike, each complete in itself, and having at the close the seed of a moral, he might work up into a series of chapters and call the book *Women Who Have Worried Me.*

He might have gone all the morning planning work he hoped to do, probably would have done so, had he not caught sight of the postman ascending the Eyrie companion-way. There was a letter for him; several in fact, but one in particular, from his Father Confessor. Paul held it in his hands for a moment; he hesitated to open it: this might seal his fate; it might be the beginning of a new career; he felt a pleasant thrill in holding the letter unopened while he speculated upon his future.

It was merely a line; it ran as follows:

MY DEAR PAUL:
Come to me without delay. I have news for you.
Your loving friend,
A. VENERABLE, S. J.

It seems that Clitheroe, hopeless of winning fame or fortune by his pen, had, in a moment of desperation appealed to Harry English for advice. As an actor of distinction and the manager of two stock companies, one of which was touring the provinces as support of a transient star of the first magnitude, it lay within his power to place a dramatic aspirant at the shortest notice and see to it that he was well bestowed.

Paul was not stage-struck; private theatricals had not turned his head; he had never for a moment desired to become a member of the Profession; but something had to be done, and as all the gates of ordinary business life seemed closed to him, he turned at last to Harry English and threw himself into the sheltering arms of that dear friend, crying "What shall I do to be saved?"

Harry, finding Paul verging upon hysteria concluded that he would, perhaps, appear to greater advantage, were he a histrionic—even though a poor one. He said as much; Paul took the matter into consideration, and while considering, appealed to his Confessor—that bosom-friend who knew him best of all. His Confessor promised to make inquiry far and wide to see if he could not discover some avenue of escape from a calling for which Paul believed he had no vocation—possibly no talent.

The note just quoted no doubt was a summons to hear the verdict for which he had been waiting with breathless anxiety. Having read the message excitedly, Clitheroe at once hastened to the Clergy House. The news that was cautiously broken to him by the Reverend Father was somewhat perplexing. With unfeigned disappointment he recounted the history of his search:

"I have not been so successful as I hoped to be. It seems that many young men are seeking positions where they may make a respectable livelihood; they are willing to accept anything that is offered to them; there are in many cases young men of some experience; hardy, accustomed to manual labor, and stronger in body than you are, my child. They could do with ease, and would gladly do what is beyond your power and is, in reality, unsuited to your station in life. My dear child, you cannot shovel coal; you cannot trundle freight upon the docks; you cannot drive a carriage for the coach companies in the city. We must look at this thing practically. You cannot keep books, for you know nothing of bookkeeping; to be sure, you might learn to keep books; but there are experienced bookkeepers now applying for positions, and applying in vain. The demand is not equal to the supply. You are fitted to do another class of work; you are fitted to adorn literature; it is a pity and a shame that there is no public provision for struggling geniuses: they are delayed, crippled, in every way discouraged by circumstances; all their aspirations are unheeded; all their aims defeated; they are actually suffered to die for lack of food and drink. They are as helpless as orphans and yet the orphan is provided for. They are surely as worthy as those who are gathered by thousands in hospitals, asylums, homes, by the local or national government and provided with food, raiment and shelter as long as they live."

The priest's face wore an air of deep concern: he resumed: "I am preaching you a long conference, my poor child; it is because I have just had my eyes opened. Searching in many quarters, I have found that your literary talent and reputation are considered an insurmountable obstacle in the way of your worldly advancement. Business men will not for a moment have a poet in their counting room, and they are no doubt right; you must look elsewhere for suitable employment. I have looked; I have searched on every hand; and I find but one opening for you and I know not what to think of it; I know not if it is to be recommended, or even to be thought of. There is a gentleman here who owns vast tracts of land in the southern part of the State; his flocks and herds wander broadcast over it; one might say that the 'Cattle upon a thousand hills are his.' He can offer you the lot of a shepherd; it will be your simple duty to lead your sheep from one vale to another in search of new pastures. At intervals your food will be brought to you. You will pass your time alone with your flock, wandering under the sun by day, and sleeping under the stars by night. A young poet might find himself in his element here! He could review his Vergil with unwonted ardor; he could even learn to play upon the pandean pipes; surely the picture is not distasteful! Such a life must necessarily be monotonous, but it should be both pleasant and peaceful!"

The priest paused, with an apologetic air. He saw all the possibilities of a pastoral life under conditions such as have made Arcadia a land of dreams. Paul was not overjoyed at the prospect of banishing himself to the brazen hills of sunburnt California, with some thousands of sheep for his constant associates and the fear of wolves, panthers, bears, rattlesnakes, centipedes, tarantulas, tramps, and heaven knows what other vermin, to enliven the days and make hideous his nights. The priest felt that unless Paul was really anxious to turn poet-peasant and shepherd his flock in the wilderness, that he had better at once abandon the thought of it.

"Look about you, my dear child," said he, sympathetically, "see if you cannot find some one who has undergone an experience of this nature, and he will be able to help you judge if you had best undertake it."

Paul's heart was faint within him; he bowed his head dutifully, but in silence.

"Go, my child," continued the priest, "go, and may God's blessing go with you; let me hear from you soon; if this place is not feasible you must go upon the stage, and then I shall pray for your success."

The Reverend Father took Clitheroe in his arms, and embraced him fervently; there were tears in the eyes of each of them as they parted a moment later.

Fate seemed to favor Paul; within a very few hours he not only heard of some one who had been through the ordeal that was awaiting him, in case he didn't abandon himself to the stage, but he met a friend who had been through it all and barely survived. He was for some months upon the southern hills; at times drenched with fog, always blown upon by the strong, bitter winds from the sea; shelterless, night and day; his sheep circling about him and staring him out of countenance with their blank eyes like smoked buttons of mother-of-pearl. He had slept upon the ground that during the night changed its temperature to such a degree the young man was now a victim of chronic rheumatism. This settled the question once and forever. Clitheroe flew to Thespian Lodge; bursting into the presence of Harry English, he cried, "I must go upon the stage, dear Harry, there is no help for it."

"Very well, my boy," exclaimed Harry, in his most charming vein; Paul began at once to take heart of grace at the sound of it: "Very well; now I wish you to select some play, one that you are particularly fond of; you will choose the character in it which pleases you most; it will be well to select a part which you have always admired, one you have longed to play; one you feel you would enjoy impersonating; study it well; I will put the play in rehearsal; I will star you for one night; if you make a hit I will give you a star engagement in a round of characters. Your reputation ought to crowd the house for some time."

"No, Harry," replied Paul mournfully, "I shall never make my appearance in this accursed town. They have starved me out of it; they have forced me to the stage where I don't belong, where I am perfectly conscious of being out of my element; neither shall I select any part to star in, nor shall I star until I have learned the art and the public is ready to make a star of me. I shall go into the country; assume a name on the bills; and begin at the foot of the ladder, in a stock company. If I am not worthy to rise—nothing can boost me up."

"Very well, my dear boy; you are quite right. I shall be sending a company into the interior next week; you shall go with it. I shall put you in charge of the manager who will, I assure you, do everything within his power to aid you—and much lies within his power. The star will be your friend, I will arrange all that. But one thing, Paul, I must insist upon, and that is your retaining your own name; it must be printed in the bills in full. Play any part that may fall to your lot—you may play it so exquisitely that it will become a feature; but, so sure as you appear under an assumed name, some one or other will recognize you, and it will be at once surmised that you are doing something that you are ashamed of, and this will be to your discredit as well as to the discredit of the profession."

"All right," sighed Clitheroe; "I'm ready to do whatever is right, and the sooner I begin to do it, the better for me."

"Dear Paul," exclaimed Mrs. English, putting her arms about him; "I've always felt that your place was on the stage. You have just the voice for it, and you will do well in juvenile business. Then you have a way of posing that is perfectly natural to you and just in the line of business for the young love. Hal, dear!" turning to her husband who was beaming on the pair, "I must see his first appearance. Only think, Paul, your name on the bill, *'His first appearance on any stage,'* and all the eyes in the house on you. We shall have you down here, presently. You need not imagine that you can hide yourself forever: but come, come, dinner is waiting. We will go to the play tonight. I want Paul to see a charming bit of acting that young Grattan Field is doing. Perhaps you have seen him this week?" Paul shook his head, as if he were a little dazed, and so he was, poor fellow. "Come, let us dine," cried Mrs. English, and they went down to dinner.

VI

Trials and Tribulations

These were anxious days for Clitheroe, but more anxious days were to come.

A British star of the old robustious school was at the head of the Dramatic Company being gathered together by Harry English. Such standard dramas as *Louis XI, Richelieu, The Merchant of Venice, The Willow Copse, Jew of Frankfort, The Cricket on the Hearth, Milky White*, etc., were at once put in rehearsal. The exquisite dramatic sketch *One Touch of Nature* was added to the list, for in it, the star has achieved a brilliant reputation. Several small parts were alloted to Paul and the marked play-books given him; or perhaps it was a folio on which his lines, with their respective cues underlined, were inscribed in a bold and legible hand.

He at once began the study of his roles; the rehearsals were of little service to him; nothing went just right, and the business of the various scenes was revised from time to time. Nobody seemed in the least interested; as for Clitheroe he could not for the life of him see how anybody should be expected to be interested. Such weary hours he had never before passed; such an empty pretence of doing something, and all to no purpose as it seemed to him was, in his eyes, time worse than wasted.

Again and again his heart failed him; again and again, he said to himself, "Why am I doing this thing? Why may I not do something else, yes, something else? My God, what can I do?"

He had been over to see Elaine, who had done her best to encourage him; he had been to see the Pompadour who had cheered him, for the time being at least, as women were very apt to do; they believed in him one and all; there was something in his manner, in his atmosphere, let us say, which strongly appealed to them. When Paul had, on a certain occasion, come forward in his dress suit and read a poem from his own pen, one lady had been heard to remark, "Isn't he perfectly lovely?" and another declared "I would like to capture him, and carry him away to a desert island." Of course they would both have grown dreadfully sick of one another, and the island could not have held them long, but who stops to think of these things when under the spell of a new and attractive personality?

The men of Clitheroe's acquaintance were not enthusiastic believers in his success upon the stage; many of them feared he had made a foolish choice of a profession, and they did not hesitate to say so; some of them declared he had not the physique; others, that the talent was wanting; all, or nearly all of them agreed that his theatrical career would speedily terminate.

The rumor of his approaching debut found its way into print. Often he was stopped upon the streets, nowadays, by those who professed to have his best interests at heart—those busy-bodies are for the most part nuisances—and they seized the occasion to call his attention to a fact which, they said, he had apparently not taken into consideration; that he was sacrificing his position in the literary world; that he was ostracising himself; society could, of course, no longer recognize him— as if the opinion of society was worth a pin's fee in his estimation and experience; he was prostituting his art; he was going straight to Hell, etc., etc., etc. It is thus that virtue warns its starving brother to beware of eating the bread which is not of their particular baking. A mad world, my masters, and no mistake!

Even the postman was a medium through which he was daily assailed. Letters of congratulations came from enthusiasts who had always believed, they said, that he had been hiding his light under a bushel; pleasant prophecies, cheering him on to noble effort and to fame and fortune; gloomy prognostications, even reproaches, were mingled with the mass of communications that flowed in from day to day.

Surely it was not an easy matter for the young man to make a conscientious study of roles quite new to him, when his friends and enemies were vying with one another to make his life a burden, and his heart was far from being in his work.

Harry English did his best to reconcile him to the situation.

"Damn one's friends!" he said in good honest English; "They are a man's greatest obstacle in life! They are, indeed! They keep one from rising by over-weighting him with good advice; if he rises in spite of them—and when he does rise he rises in spite of them—they fawn upon him and would drag him down again in their frantic efforts to reach his level. The man who has many friends is pretty heavily handicapped." The fine indignation of the hearty manager was a handsome picture, and Mrs. English looked fondly at her lord, while Paul once more took heart.

"Never mind, my boy," said Harry, "we'll have you out of this in a few days from now. You were right in refusing to make your debut here; these people would have hounded you to death—damned if they wouldn't!"

In a few days Clitheroe was ready to depart for the scene of action. He had made the acquaintance of the various members of the company; that is he had met them—stage people never really know one another, and for that matter, it is a wise dispensation of Providence that they do not. He had found a friend in the star, who seemed inclined to take the debutant under his protection, and who in odd moments, when they fell into conversation, gave him such hints as to his conduct and treatment of his fellow-professionals as served him in good stead a little later on, and spared him much uneasiness.

VII

Among the Mummers

In a small theatre, for the dedication of which the young poet had written an open address, on a very limited stage, before an audience select, though provincial, Paul Clitheroe made his first appearance on any stage. The fact was officially announced upon the bill of the play; it was made more conspicuous upon the huge posters that stared at him from every street corner in the town; it was even the subject of polite comment in the local press, and was telegraphed briefly to the chief theatrical organ in the Misty City—an organ which contained the play-bill of every place of amusement in town, together with no little reading matter of considerable literary merit.

All this should have made him realize that he was of some slight importance in the cast of characters at the theatre where he was engaged, and the fact should have consoled, if it did not inspire him. It had no such effect upon him. He realized that he knew nothing of the art of acting, save in theory; that what little experience he may have enjoyed in amateur theatricals was a hindrance rather than an aid to success. He not only had everything to learn, but he had something to unlearn.

A few friends, residents of the town, gathered about him, and offered such encouragement as lay within their power; to all things and to everybody he seemed stolidly indifferent. He was out of his element and he was well aware of the fact; but it was not his fault—at least he felt certain that it was through no fault of his that he was where he was, and the conviction seemed likely to embitter him; therefore he conned his lines as a convict treads a mill. When the evening of his debut arrived, he was calmly indifferent to his fate. There was in reality more anxiety among his fellow players on that momentous occasion, than he betrayed or was even conscious of. When he was about to make his entrance—Act 1st, Scene 2d—in company with a group of old stagers, they spoke words of cheer which he did not heed, even if he heard them; his manner was as self-possessed as that of any one in the company. The truth is that he scorned everybody in the house at that moment; indeed, it might be said that he scorned everybody in the world: he was utterly indifferent to the cloud of witnesses beyond the flaring girdle of the footlights. The thousands of staring eyes, all more or less critical, and perhaps not a dozen pairs of them truly sympathetic, did not trouble him; he took no heed of the applause, though he was dimly conscious of it as he passed down to his allotted position on the stage; he heard his cue and recited his lines easily and naturally; the leading lady, who was in reality the daughter of the star and who had taken a deep interest in him from the first, kept him near her; piloted him through the scene with a gracious concern, and at times whispered in his ear a word or two of cheer that doubtless aided him to retain a seemingly unnatural composure.

There was one moment and one moment only when his head began to swim and his heart to beat audibly, and he would gladly, had it been possible, have faded from view; this was when he was seized by the leading lady and dragged down upon the footlights—the business of the scene called for this perilous predicament—and then a brief altercation took place between the lady and himself. It was all over in a moment, but that moment was one of great trial, and the memory of it sometimes woke him from his dreams in a cold sweat. Again, in dreams he would find himself hovering over the flames of the footlights; again the faces of the auditors resolved themselves into one monstrous staring countenance, a face as large as the house itself, set thick with unwinking eyes; again he would feel as if he were about to lose his balance and plunge headlong into space, a sacrifice to the devouring curiosity of a heartless world.

Clitheroe recovered himself; the pallor and the chill were quickly followed by a feverish heat: he was glad when the act was over. To be sure there were three others to follow; but in some of these he had little or nothing to do; and meanwhile he could climb the ladder that led to the door of his stuffy little dressing room, and sit in about three hundred cubic feet of solitude—of solitude which was red-hot if it was nothing else.

The first night was over. In the last scene of the last act, before the star was about to enter upon the final agonies of his agonizing evening, he turned to Clitheroe and said—"My boy, you may write to your friends that they need not worry themselves about you; you have done very well indeed." This was a consolation, but it gave the debutant no particular pleasure. The various members of the company were no doubt earnest in the expression of their good wishes; they must have realized that the addition of a poet to their ranks, a poet not without an enviable

CHARLES WARREN STODDARD

reputation, a young gentleman who had been pronounced one of the most popular in town, was, to say the least, nothing to be ashamed of.

Clitheroe accepted their congratulations, and, donning citizen attire, strolled out of the dark passage that lies between the world of fancy and the world of fact, and found the fact hardly less creditable than the fancy.

That night he was sleepless; he wrote a half dozen letters to his intimates, of whom we shall know more presently; to Elaine, to Jack, now far away in Venice, to Little Mama in care of Calvin Falsom. He longed very much to write to Grattan Field; now if ever they should have been the closest friends; now if ever they two might have joined hands and been in complete sympathy. He could hardly resist a strong impulse to write to Grattan Field, and tell him of his entrance on a new career. Having retired and finding that he could not sleep, he arose again and penned a long and affectionate letter to this quondam chum. He made a careless and playful allusion to a childish spat that had for a time estranged them, and then related at some length the experience of the last few weeks, and tried to give expression to the emotions, all so new, which now possessed him. Having freed his mind and heart, he returned to his pillow and slept heavily until late in the morning following.

On the morning following he was awakened by a tap at the door; enter the leading comedian of a company playing at the opposition theatre: he was, a little later, a star of the second or third magnitude in London. He had come to congratulate Clitheroe upon his successful debut: this was certainly a kind condescension on the part of the comedian. Perhaps the fact that Paul for some time previous had been the subject of numerous newspaper items on the adoption of the stage as a profession, may have had some softening influence on the heart of the comedian; the breast of the comedian is not, as a rule, overflowing with the milk of human kindness. He cannot afford to be kind within the limited range of his acquaintances. He knows nothing of society, in the general acceptation of the term; usually he reads nothing outside his play books and the dramatic journals, or the theatrical notices in the daily press. He is apt to see nothing, at any rate nothing that is of interest to him, save only those portions of the plays in which he himself appears, with an occasional glimpse at some play in the neighboring temple of the drama. He has his satellites, the type of young man who hangs about the theatre, and is proud to be seen walking on the fashionable side of the afternoon pavement with the Mummer, whose colossal portrait richly tinted and wrought to the pitch of manly beauty, adorns the high fences and the fire walls of the city.

The comedian in question introduced himself rather awkwardly. It is a singular fact that, in most cases, the thespian who charms the public with his ease and elegance, when impersonating the society swell in the marble halls of the modern comedy is very apt to be quite unpresentable, when stripped of all his lines and his elaborate stage setting. In the recitation of dialogue two well-drilled dolts may make a very creditable impression; the intellect that scintillates in sparkling repartee is apt to "lag superfluous" not on, but off the stage. The comedian in his off-hand, but rather patronizing fashion, assured Clitheroe, that, with study and experience, he could no doubt, in the course of time become an ornament to the profession. It was greatly to his credit that he was at his ease; that he did not swing upon his hips; or seem overburdened with hands and feet. He spoke his lines clearly, also. The comedian, having paid Paul an honest compliment in a commonplace manner, withdrew. His exit was above criticism; indeed, Clitheroe had long before discovered in his intercourse with the various members of the dramatic profession that they usually made admirable entrances and exits.

An early mail brought him a copy of the Dramatic Journal issued in the Misty City: glancing through its columns, his eye fell upon a telegraphic dispatch giving in a few lines an account of his debut: it announced that "barring the slight nervousness natural to debutants his first appearance was creditable." Several letters of congratulation arrived by a later post. None of those gave him any pleasure. The truth is, that his heart was not in his work. He had resolved that he would stick to his profession until he found an opening in some other field, which though it might not be any more to his taste, would at least permit him to retire from the gaze of the public.

He was now no longer able to walk the streets without finding himself an object of interest in the eyes of a host of strangers. He seemed to especially attract the attention of half-grown boys; the bootblacks, his gallery critics, were his ardent admirers; the newsboys smiled recognition as he passed them; the waiters at the restaurants where he refreshed himself, paid him such special attentions that he soon discovered they were hoping to receive their reward in "passes" to the play. His barber, who was eager to draw him into conversation for the edification of the patrons in the adjoining chairs, was effusive in his professional attentions. When he left the theatre at night he usually found a group of idlers attracted by the light that hung above the stage entrance, as are the dazzled moths, and some of those were ever ready to accept and return the slightest recognition.

One youth had fastened himself upon the attention of Clitheroe and would in no wise be cast aside: he was a constant attendant at the play, and Paul soon began to recognize his face among the sitters in the stalls. If the actor went to the edge of the curtain to cast a side-glance upon the audience, the eyes of his unknown friend caught his, and shortly forced a smile. He was a devotee, and Paul was his idol. He would follow the player to his lodgings, pressing a thousand little kindly attentions upon him; he was never so happy as when Paul would consent to accept a late supper at his hands, and permit him to share the midnight oyster and musty ale which usually followed the labors of the evening. He was a bright and wellbred lad who filled a clerkship dutifully during the day, but whose one pleasure in life seemed to be to spend his leisure hours in the society of his idol, before and behind the foot-lights.

"Is it for this," cried Clitheroe, "I have pillared myself before the eyes of the world? A bait for critics to nibble at; the admiration of some, the scorn of others; with no hope of privacy so long as I am posted upon the fences and dead walls of the town I play in! Had I sought publicity, I would have found myself in the seventh heaven—but to have it forced upon me—ah, how different that is!"

He went to his chamber very early in the morning, and stayed there until the hour of rehearsal called him forth. Sometimes he felt as if he was stripped naked before the world; as if his secret thoughts were known to the curious public. The idea preyed upon him, and made him nervous and ill. Even the flattering tributes of the unknown correspondents were not balm to such wounds as notoriety gave him.

VIII

Hard Lines

One fact was soon made manifest to all, namely, that Paul Clitheroe was not likely to end his days upon the stage, unless they ended speedily. He felt that they would end speedily unless he could make an honorable exit and retire to private life.

He was playing in a small town; the bill was changed frequently; this necessitated incessant study and daily rehearsals.

"They call us players," said he one day overcome with weariness, "they call us players, and yet my work begins when I waken upon my pillow in the morning and goes on until I close my eyes in the small hours of the morning following: it never, never ends; I don't see how it can ever end!" and he fetched a great despairing sigh such as would have touched the hearts of his auditors, had he been before the foot-lights at that moment.

It was his custom to go to sleep with his "part" tucked under his pillow; his first thought upon waking was, do I know my lines? With a heavy heart he would draw the play-book, or the manuscript of his role from its hiding place; he would pass his hand slowly down the page until his eye fell upon his cue; then he would rack his brain for the speech that was to follow; sometimes he would recall it; often he could not, and every moment of hesitation but added to his discouragement.

When he had been through his lines so that they were tolerably familiar, he would rise and make his toilet. At the breakfast table he renewed his task, for it would soon be time for rehearsal; his one consolation when he entered the theatre was to find that not a soul in the company, save only the star and his daughter the leading lady, were any more familiar with the text of the play which was to be produced that evening, than Paul himself.

For two or three indescribable hours the company stumbled through the several roles; if it was a drama that was in rehearsal, there was nothing dramatic suggested; if a comedy, it was utterly wanting in humor and sparkle; if a farce, there was no fun in it. The stage business and the situations were a source of much vexatious discussion, and after some hours of active misery the stage was deserted until evening,—yet no, not quite deserted, for the scene painters and the stage carpenters were always busy and not infrequently the setting of a play was finished but a few moments before the rising of the curtain.

Clitheroe had cues for breakfast, cues for luncheon, and cues warmed over for dinner; he chewed the cud of his cue from morning till night; and of all the unpalatable dainties that were ever forced upon him he found these the least digestible. He went early to the theatre in the evening and was often dressed for his part soon after seven o'clock; he was not to face the audience until an hour later; possibly he was not *on* in the first act at all, but his companions were there almost as early as he, and the scene was a busy one, for each of the players was walking to and fro about the stage, or they were gathered in the stuffy little "Green Room," or hidden away in their box-like dressing rooms, still studying their lines.

There was an ambitious youth, who, though young, was no novice, and he might be found strutting the stage, in the afternoons, reciting his lines over and over to empty benches. At these hours, he could tear a passion to tatters without disturbing any one, for the stage carpenters are a hardened lot and quite used to this seeming waste of energy. Were Clitheroe in love with his profession, he would no doubt have found it profitable to develop his lungs and test his voice, and practice his struts and his poses, in this fashion. He would have gloried in having the stage all to himself—the painters and the carpenters one learns to pass unnoticed—in keeping it as long as he chose; in working up his scenes until he had won noiseless thunders of applause from imaginary audiences wrought to the highest pitch of enthusiasm.

But Paul would none of it. The odors of the play-house, the unmistakable aroma, compounded of gas, turpentine, dry-wash paint, and the dead air of an ill-ventilated house, had no charms for him. Had he been born to the purple of the player-king, these very odors would have been as sweet as incense in his nostrils.

The play was ended; the curtain was rung up upon the deserted auditorium; he donned his citizen's garb and sought out the small bulletin board where the notices of the rehearsals for the day following were posted: here he found the plays announced, with the cast of characters appended. The prompter was on hand to distribute the alloted parts. Sometimes Clitheroe was cast for a role the assumption of which should not have been attempted until after weeks of arduous study; he should have analyzed and absorbed the part, carefully considering all its elements and fixing them in his mind; the character should have become his second nature for the time being. How was this possible when at 11:30 P.M. he saw himself doomed to assume a character, which very likely lay quite out of his line, and to appear for the rehearsal at 10:00 o'clock the next morning? On the evening of that day he was to recite the lines, not a word of which was familiar to him, and thus, in four and twenty hours he was to crowd the experience of a little lifetime. The day following, it was more than likely that he would find himself recast in another play—possibly two of them, for he sometimes played in the drama or comedy with which the evening's entertainment opened, as well as in the farce which closed it.

Over his midnight chop and mellow ale he read his new part for the first time. If his particular admirer was with him, as was not infrequently the case, he would perhaps memorize a scene, his friend giving out the cues to which Paul made the proper responses. There was a kind of pleasure in this; he rather enjoyed it; as for that companion, he was perfectly delighted. He would have gladly prolonged the supper and the study hour, but the cafe was sure to close, and they would find themselves forced to adjourn to the street.

Alone in his room, worn out with the anxieties of the day, Clitheroe could not sleep: he must at least attempt to master his lines before retiring. O! how his eyes dropped, his head ached, and his heart sank! The Star, who spoke encouragingly to him at intervals, once said:

"Has it been your custom from your youth up to memorize the poems you have liked, and take pleasure in reciting them aloud?"

Clitheroe was about to answer that he believed he had not done much of that sort of thing, when the Star continued:

"Have you gathered your friends about you on every possible occasion and played at them? Have you cornered them, if necessary, and insisted on their listening to you, whether they would or no? And has it seemed to you that the one thing that would make life worth living was for you to become a great actor, playing star-parts before wildly enthusiastic audiences, and that you would ultimately do this, or die?"

Paul replied modestly, that such had not been the case with him. "Then what"—exclaimed the Star—who was a star of the good old blustering and explosive school, and who never spared his words— "then what in Hell are you doing here?"

Clitheroe colored, feeling somehow, as if he were guilty of trespassing, he replied:

"I am trying to make a living; it is positively necessary that I do something in order to earn my bread; I have tried to write, as you know well enough, but my pen cannot support me; I have looked everywhere, and offered my services to all sorts of people, willing to do anything that might be my allotted task; my friends have made earnest efforts in my behalf, yet the one sole avenue of escape from slow starvation that was open to me was the stage—and that is why I am here. I hope you will forgive me," concluded Paul, with a smile that was humorously apologetic.

The Star took him by the arm and they walked up the street, the observed of all observers: he was no longer uncomfortable; one soon becomes accustomed to being stared at: as they walked, Paul said to his now very amiable companion:

"Was it your custom to 'play-act' when you were yet a child?"

"My dear boy"—replied he heartily—"I nearly bored my friends to death. I was always studying new parts: I imagined myself Hamlet, Romeo, Macbeth,—a thousand different heroes; nothing lay out of my reach; I was equal to any role, whether tragic or comic; I aped the gait and postures of the actors I idolized. I drilled my playmates in dramas which we produced in barns; I was proprietor, manager, prompter, call-boy, property-man, costumer, everything under the sun: I was the Star—of course I am always the star—and I grew up with my eye fixed upon the stage, and my determination to become an actor was never for a moment shaken: I ran away with a troupe of strolling players; was captured and well flogged for it: I ran away again, and then my wise parents concluded to foster whatever talent I might possess, and I secured an engagement in a respectable theatre where I served some years of apprenticeship. Ah, my dear Clitheroe, it is a hard profession you have been forced into; from the bottom of my heart I pity you."

"But since I have been forced into it, how shall I make the most of it? Can't you advise me what is best to do?"

The Star's manner grew soft and gentle: "Have you a good study?" he inquired.

"Alas, no. I have the worst study in the world; and what makes it doubly distressing, is that I have no confidence in myself; I distrust my memory; I am always turning again to my lines to make sure of them."

"Bad, all bad; very bad indeed: you had better a thousand times look well through your part, and throw the book away. Never refer to your book after you come to the theatre at night. The child who does not push the prop from him will never learn to walk. The prompter should be able to tide you over."

"But there is so much studying to be done; so many parts to learn and we play most of them but once!"

"Yes, you will never have harder work to do than you are doing just now. Indeed, you may find yourself a member of some company where a play will have a very long run, and having become familiar with your part, you will have no further studying to do. Then, if you are with a company that is on the road, you are sure to repeat your parts very often, and you will have the opportunity of seeing many cities and different parts of the country; perhaps you may even make a tour of the globe; would not that interest you?"

"Yes, yes indeed! But I would rather see different lands and peoples as I have already seen them; wandering at my pleasure, hither and yon, and choosing such companions as I found most attractive; society and publicity were not forced upon me when I was a foreign correspondent and yet there was little money in that! O, money! money! how I hate the necessity which compels me to seek it!"

"You will never make money in our profession unless you rise in it; and then you will probably not keep it."

The Star was rather abrupt, but Clitheroe felt the undeniable truth of his statement.

"I think I could keep money if I had it!" responded he.

"Well, then you must make up your mind to work for it—and to work with all your might and main. An actor who hopes to reach the top of his profession must not only have talent, voice, figure, health, energy and application—he should have a steam engine at the base of his brain."

"My God!" exclaimed Clitheroe involuntarily; he was beginning to realize how impossible it would be for him to even dream of success upon the stage.

"You say you have a bad study?" rejoined the Star, perhaps hoping to help the boy a little, and not really meaning to discourage him at all. "I have found it a great aid"—he continued, "when I have been forced to acquire a part in haste, to bind my forehead with a towel dipped in cold water; this keeps my eyes open at night, when otherwise I should fall asleep in my chair. I study at night and go over my lines the first thing after waking in the morning!"

"So do I," said Paul, "but such headaches, and such aching eyes, and a desire for sleep that overwhelms me at times! Well, I'll try the wet towel this very night and thank you for the suggestion."

They parted—Clitheroe to wander where he had often wandered of late, by the river-bank a little below the town. The dismantled hull of some craft, once manned by argonauts, and long since deserted, was deeply bedded in the soft ooze of the shore; a stationary gang-plank afforded easy access to the deck of the hulk; the old castaway was sometimes utilized as a temporary dock, but it was for the most part deserted. Often and often had Paul wandered thither to sun himself in solitude. Here, hidden behind the bulwarks, he felt comparatively secluded, and he would pore with listless eyes over the hateful text he was endeavoring to memorize. Sometimes he was spied out by youthful swimmers, or straggling tramps, and routed from his chosen retreat; but frequently he was left to himself for hours, and his study was unbroken save by those lapses into reverie, and reverie that was growing less cheerful day by day.

Again and again, he had put the question to himself in all earnestness; "If I were the greatest tragedian in the world; if I had name, fame, fortune at my command; if I were the idol of the public, and had a whole nation at my feet—yet had always to be strutting before these foot-lights, surrounded by the class of men and women of which the profession is, unhappily, largely composed—would it be worth my while to struggle on year after year unto the end?" And his answer was always the same: "No it would not!"

And then—"How long before the public would weary of me, and the newer star would crowd me out of my orbit? How long before the idol would be shattered—stoned by the very ones who had done it homage? No, a thousand times no! Sooner would I cast myself into that sluggish stream and end all, than drag out a miserable existence that offers me nothing but oblivion at the end!"

More than once, as Paul in deep dejection had looked down upon the river flowing so near him, he had paused for a moment—as if balancing upon the edge of a resolve—and then turned suddenly and hurriedly from the spot. A moment more, a second longer, and he would have ended his life of misery, then and there. But he was spared for a better sacrifice. With dogged determination he strode back into the town; felt again the scrutinizing eyes of the public resting upon him—the public who so little suspected the anguish that was gnawing at his vitals.

He played his part at night, played it as well perhaps as any of the minor people in the art played theirs: was not especially glad when the play was over, for that meant merely a change of lines, and so he would return to his chamber after midnight, to don his turban of damp towels and resume his endless task.

IX

FROM BAD TO WORSE

For some weeks Paul Clitheroe had struggled manfully with fate. Wind and tide were against him, and he was making for a far distant port whose beacon lights were not yet in view. Neither did he set much store by aught he was likely to find there, when he should have taken in sail and dropped anchor at the end of the voyage.

Many members of the profession offered him encouragement, by letter or by word of mouth. His circle of acquaintances was increasing day by day. He was a conspicuous character. His photographs and autographs were in demand; newspaper correspondents were seeking introductions to him and writing him up in a very agreeable fashion. He was on the high road to success, the envy of many of his fellows; some of whom, inspired by a spirit of jealousy, were not above throwing obstacles in his path and dropping in his hearing remarks calculated to wound his feelings, but for all these inevitable consequences of the peculiar circumstances which surrounded him, he cared nothing. In the beginning he had resolved that he would start at the foot of the ladder and work his way up, if it were possible for him to do so. Later, he said to himself, "If anything else offers, if I can see any avenue of escape from this miserable existence I shall seize the opportunity and quietly retire, no matter what my friends or the world may think."

So it came to pass, after long and patient waiting, that he had a three days' leave of absence, during which he was to visit his friends in the Misty City. He took with him the text of a half-dozen parts for which he was cast and which he was to play during the week following his return. His friend the Star completed his engagement and departed. The stock company had been busy reviving old plays, comedies and farces, such as confirmed theatregoers are bound to see at intervals. A pretty and vivacious Prima Donna was delighting the public in a late comic opera success; it was during the last week of her engagement that Paul was permitted to leave the theatre for a few days. He had played a new role during the early part of her engagement, that of prompter; and the experience had added nothing to his love of, or respect for the profession. He rejoiced mightily when he heard that he might absent himself for some days previous to the appearance of an Irish Comedian whose name was a household word in three continents, and who was to follow the Prima Donna.

Paul packed his valise—with his heart in it. He had begun to think that he could never again take interest in anything, but he took interest in this, and found his spirits rising rapidly.

All the way down the river, on the homeward voyage, he pored over his play-books. He read the several roles in the series of Irish Comediettas as far as he was to appear in them, to ascertain if he was likely to distinguish himself in any one of them. Alas! not one interested him in the smallest degree.

He resolved that he would not worry himself about them until the last moment. If he had many times before learned a part and played it within four and twenty hours, he could surely do it again. He would during these four days abandon himself to the joy of a brief reunion with his friends; never had they seemed dearer to him than at this moment.

What friends they were; pals, most of them, whether male or female. There was the queenly Miss Juno who he called "Jack" for short and for the sake of the jolly fellowship they shared.

"If only Jack were here," he said to himself, "if only Jack were here, I would fly to her at once, and what a lark we should have!"

But Jack was in Venice, and he had begun to think that they were never to meet again.

"Elaine the fair, Elaine the lovable," he was sure to see and the thought of her was a joy to him. Perhaps by this time "Little Mama" the Vanishing Lady who had cast her spell over him and developed a phase in his character undreamed of until her advent—perhaps they might meet again! And then he would dine with the Pompadour and the lively coterie at the Hotel de France; he would once more be supremely happy.

When Paul had departed on his theatrical venture, he had not given up his lodgings at the Eyrie. He felt certain of his salary: he did not feel certain of his future. So long as he was on the stage, his salary was likely to be sufficient for all his needs, and he could pay his rent in the Eyrie, and feel that his effects were safer in the hands of his landlady than if he had packed and stored them where moth and rust, mice and dust are very apt to corrupt.

So he returned to the Eyrie, and found himself once more at home. How beautiful it seemed to him to be there! Everything was in perfect order; it was as if he had not been away at all. O, why need he be away? Why could he not stay there forever, and do enough writing to just cover his expenses, and never again be forced to face the unfeeling world? As he asked himself this question, over and over again, he was half inclined to complain of his hard lot; yet he had never really done so in his heart; he bowed to fate with becoming resignation; sighed a little oftener than usual; was more hungry at times, and more depressed; that was all, and of all this his friends for the most part had no knowledge.

On the morning after his re-appearance in the Misty City, he took a leisurely turn through the streets; he was thoroughly enjoying his freedom. Acquaintances were greeting him cordially on every hand. The local press had announced his arrival in town, and he seemed to be an object of unusual interest in the eyes of the public at large. He ascertained that the Bohemians at the Hotel de France were scattered hither and yon; that nothing was quite as it had been, only a few weeks before. It seemed almost as if everything had changed during his absence, and that, after all, perhaps the best thing for him to do was to go back to the stage and stick there, to the bitter end.

With various emotions, he wandered about the streets, or locked himself in his lodgings, seeking consolation and solitude. His anticipated delight seemed to be evaporating; after all perhaps it was only a mirage. He was turning matters over in his mind during the long lonely stroll in the suburbs when he chanced to meet one of the newspaper fraternity, item-hunting, no doubt, and they naturally fell into conversation: said he, of the press, to Paul, after the usual commonplaces:

"How do you like the stage as a profession?"

"I hate it," replied Paul impulsively,—"but you are not interviewing me, are you?"

"Certainly not; what we say is in strict confidence—unless you would like to be interviewed. It would give me the greatest pleasure to interview you and might not hurt you professionally, you know."

"It might not hurt me, but would it help me? Help is what I stand most in need of, help of the right sort," said Paul a little sadly.

"What kind of help do you want?"

"I wish to leave the stage; I wish never to see it or hear of it again; I would rather bury myself alive somewhere, anywhere, than to stand at the very top of the profession!"

"I wonder at that: there are no end of fellows who envy you, not only on the stage, but off it; your literary reputation, your social position, your Eyrie, your everything—and yet you don't seem to be happy or satisfied."

"I am neither happy nor satisfied. Sometimes I wonder if I was ever either satisfied or happy."

The press-man looked puzzled; for a time they walked on together in silence. He seemed inclined to say something to Clitheroe, but for some reason hesitated. At last he ventured to ask:

"You think you would be willing to accept any position open to you?"

"Most assuredly; I believe I would accept anything offered me at this moment!"

"I wonder if you would care to go to the office of the 'Saturday Matinee' and ask if the vacancy which they have been advertising far and wide has been filled. I don't know what the vacancy is!"

"I don't care what it is; I will go there at once, you may be sure of that!" They parted, Paul hastened to the office in question.

The "Saturday Matinee" was an alleged literary periodical, which in its day had been the brilliant organ of a company of extremely clever Bohemians. It had long since passed out of their hands, and fallen into dotage. A lady of wealth, with literary ambition, had purchased the dilapidated plant, and placed it in the hands of her husband, who was business manager and silent editor. She wrote stories, reviews, a lively social column, in which she handled rather smartly the society circles which she held in little esteem. He did the editorials with his fist. This was the man to whom it was Clitheroe's lot to apply for a position. When he inquired for the Editor, he was informed that the gentleman was not present. It was very uncertain at what hour he would be present: Paul was advised to state his business, and drop in again by and by. The business stated, he promised to call later in the day. This was Friday, an unlucky day in which to begin a new venture thought Paul, as he descended the unswept stairs leading to a narrow side street.

Toward evening the youth again presented himself; he hardly dared to hope that his day of deliverance was at hand. The office, an ill-furnished one, looked gloomier than ever. The editor was not in. But a man who was his spokesman told Paul, somewhat brusquely, that he might call at noon on the day following and receive a definite reply to his application. The day following would be Saturday; he could not learn his fate before noon. In case his services were accepted in the office of the "Saturday Matinee" he had resolved to remain in the Misty City; if he found no opening up that dingy bystreet, he was to sail at four o'clock and resume the unceasing study of his roles. He had not the slightest idea in what capacity he was to be employed, in case the engagement was offered him, but this did not trouble him seriously; he was perfectly serious when he declared that he would rather do anything under the sun than remain upon the stage.

Promptly at noon on the day following, Clitheroe inquired for the editor of the "Saturday Matinee" and to his surprise discovered that the man with whom he had already had two interviews, and whom he had supposed to be the business manager, was the editor himself; he had not felt authorized to make any engagement with Paul until his wife had been duly consulted, and he had won her consent. She concluded that the youth might be made use of in more ways than one, and so he was informed that he might enter upon his duties on the following Monday morning. He was to receive an insignificant salary, but he resolved that a crust of bread in an attic with four walls between him and the world he loathed, was preferable to sock and buskin at any price. The bargain was struck at once, and Paul went forth rejoicing, or trying to rejoice at his alleged deliverance.

With utmost haste he telegraphed to his manager that unforeseen circumstances would necessitate his immediate withdrawal from the company. His play-books he returned by express. To the youth who had become his almost constant companion he wrote a letter begging that his trunks might be packed and forwarded as soon as convenient, and the hotel clerk might be informed that he no longer required his room; his late manager, who was somewhat in his debt would settle for the same—and so ended his theatrical career.

It transpired that Paul's chief duty in the office of the "Saturday Matinee" was to keep a set of books which he was to exhibit to the wife of the editor weekly, submitting himself the while to a rigid cross-examination concerning the affairs of the office.

In those books, Clitheroe entered the moneys that went out, and kept an unsullied page for the moneys that were expected to come in; but they never to his knowledge came. In his off-hours—how many of them they were—he sat in the office and announced to numerous creditors that the editor was not in. He fancied himself playing another role, for the character he assumed in that office was as unreal as any he had ever in his life enacted. He was recommended to relieve the monotony of the day by taking the bucolic directory, and addressing innumerable wrappers to provincial trades-people throughout the land;

back numbers of the "Saturday Matinee"—the office was lumbered with them—were folded in those wrappers, and at intervals when he could be spared, that is when the editor was on hand to announce his own absence, he bravely bore armfuls of these devoted papers to the post-office and deposited them with a sigh of relief. He was informed, as delicately as might be expected, considering the source, that if the "spirit moved him," the columns of the "Saturday Matinee" were graciously and gratuitously open to him. On several occasions he felt constrained to offer a contribution, for it seemed not improbable that he might pay some penalty if he refused. On several occasions he had been sent to the literary boudoir of the editor's wife, with a note requesting money enough to square the bills incurred in the composing room. She responded, of course, for had she not done so the paper would have come to an end that very night, but Paul was witness of her indignation and he did not relish these interviews.

Clitheroe's only tolerable hours in the office were when the editor was actually absent; when he could sit at the table where day after day and week after week, he addressed wrappers to the world at large: he had learned to do this mechanically; often his thoughts were thousands of miles from the dreary office—yes, as far away as Venice. Would it not, on the whole, have been pleasanter starving in Venice—starving physically—than to be starving spiritually in this new captivity?

Of course his friends were shrugging their shoulders over his predicaments. His unpracticability, his want of application, his vagaries, were freely commented upon. They, the critical friends, were ready to wash their hands of him; it were vain to imagine anything could be done for, or with, such a dreamer as he.

He was being left more and more to himself every day. How gladly he would have returned to seek distraction among the merry men at the Hotel de France—were they still making merry there? But no: even Harry English could not quite disguise his disappointment at Paul's unceremonious exit from his company. The poor fellow was drifting helpless and alone—alone as he had ever been more or less alone. In a certain sense this was always the case with him.

For years, like the snail, he had, as it were, carried his house about with him; his home, all that he knew of home, was wherever he chanced to pause for a time, and he had acquired the knack—the art, if you will dignify it by that title—of easy domestication; so it came to pass that in Bloomsbury, or Fitz Roy Square, he felt and acted like a Londoner:

he was jolly, after a half-foreign fashion, in the Latin Quarter—though how he could feel at home in Paris is past finding out; he acquired a Venetian languor on the Riva Schiavoni, and was wedded to the Narghiles of Cairo and Damascus. Most of all, it may be said, he was at his ease under the palms of the Pacific. He was, no doubt, imbued with sentiment—how few people truly are; how many sport a spurious article and know nothing of the genuine! Whether he had enough or too much sentiment is for you to judge, when you know him better. He knew himself well enough, and many a time when cruising aimlessly in the southern seas, he had gathered by the shore a shell, or in some native grass-thatched village a curio, and had brought these with him as a precious souvenir—certain that the day was sure to come when in the long silence of his summer, or the short sharp gloom of his winter days, only to hear the wail of the savage Islander, piercing the air, would thrill his heart with emotion; only to see the sleek dark forms as they glistened in the spray of the reef, silhouettes on a golden ground, done in Byzantine simplicity, would dazzle and dim his eyes.

He was at ease in most every phase of life, and not even a predicament could distract him; camping among cannibals, basking in the favor of the Cardinal Prince, starving in Bohemia or with the holy missionaries in far-off places, feasting with Eastern potentates or disporting with thespian stars or coryphees were alike to him, as far as the eternal fitness of things was concerned. Yet there was a natural tendency to method, that made it easy for him to drop into a rut. Perhaps after all he could get used to his new life and live it out.

X

Balm of Hurt Wounds

The cloud which had been gathering over Paul Clitheroe grew darker and darker. The editor of the "Saturday Matinee" was at odds with the wife who was growing weary of a constant drain upon her purse, and gave with a grudging hand. It was Paul's duty to pay off the compositors on Saturday nights: sometimes when this was accomplished there was not enough left over to cover his own account with the office, small as that was, and he had not the moral courage to make complaint, or let the fact be known.

He was scrimping in every way; his case was growing desperate. The books, the pictures, the bric-a-brac so precious in his eyes, he was loath to part with; moreover, he was well aware that if he were to trundle his effects down to an auction-room they would not bring him enough to cover his expenses for a single week. "Better to starve in the midst of my household gods," thought he, "than to part with them for the sake of prolonging this misery." The situation was in some respects seriocomic. While he seemed to have everything, he really had almost nothing; he was in a certain sense at the mercy of his friends and dependent upon them.

As the dinner hour approached, Paul was called upon to make choice of the character of his table-talk; there were several standing invitations to dine at the houses of old friends, and these were a boon to him, for at such houses the homeless fellow felt much at home. There were special invitations, sometimes an embarrassing profusion of them—all kindly, some persistent, and some even imperative; thus the dinner was a fixed fact; the mood alone was to be consulted in his choice of a table and after all how much of the success of a dinner depends upon the mood of the diner!

Paul's income was uncertain; while he had written much, and traveled much as a special correspondent, he had never regularly connected himself with any journal, and he knew nothing of the routine of office-work. Sometimes, I may say not infrequently, he could not write at all; yet his pen was his only source of revenue, and often he was without a copper to his credit. He was, therefore, constrained to dine sumptuously with friends, when he would have found a solitary salad a sweet alternative, and independence far more acceptable. The state of the exchequer was very often alarming, and his predicament might have cast a stronger man into the depths; but Paul could fast without complaint, when necessary, for he had fasted often; and, to confess the truth, he would much rather have fasted on and on, than parted with any of the little souvenirs that made his surroundings charming in spite of his privations. The friends who loved and fondled him were wont to send messengers to his door with gifts of flowers, books, pictures and the like, when soup-tickets would have been more serviceable, though by no means more acceptable. It had happened to him more than once, that having failed to break his fast—for he had a judicious horror of debt, born of bitter experience—he received at a late hour as tokens of sincere interest in his welfare, scarf pins, perfumery and scented soap; or it may have been a silk handkerchief bearing the richly wrought monogram of the happy but hungry recipient. At any rate these testimonials of his popularity were never edible. Was this hard luck? He went from one swell dinner to another, day after day, with never so much as a crumb between meals. It of course made some difference to him—this prolonged abstinence—but fortunately, or unfortunately, the effect upon him mentally, morally and physically was hardly visible to the naked eye.

He had a dress coat of the strictly correct type, which he had worn but a few times; he had lectured in it; once or twice, he had recited poems in it to the audiences of admiring lady friends. It was of no use to him now, and he felt that he should never need it again. On the street below him was a small shop, kept by the customary Israelite. Again and again, Paul had noted the sun-faded frock-coat swinging from a hook over the sidewalk in front of this shop; he had said, "I will take this coat to him; it is a costly garment; divide the original price of it by the number of times I have worn it and I find it has cost me about ten dollars an evening. Perhaps this old-clothes dealer will pay me a fair price for it; Jew though he be, he may be possessed of the heart of a Christian!"

Alas and alack! All of Clitheroe's sufferings could be traced to the cool, calculating hardness of the Christian's heart. Probably it was prejudice alone that caused him to trust the Christian, and distrust the Jew.

From day to day he passed the shop, striving to muster courage enough to enter and propose his bargain. At first he had imagined the dealer offering him but ten dollars for the coat—it had cost him a goodly sum; a little later he concluded that ten dollars was too little for any one to offer him; he might take twenty; a day later thirty seemed to him a probable offer, and shortly after he imagined himself consenting to receive fifty dollars, since the coat was in such admirable repair.

One day he took it to the dealer; he was not cordially welcomed by the man in shirt sleeves, with whom of late he had held innumerable imaginary conversations. The shop was extremely small and dark; the odor of dead garments pervaded it. With an earnest and kindly glance, Paul invited the sympathy of Abraham the son of Moses who was the son of Isaac; he saw nothing but speculation in those eyes. His coat was examined and tossed aside, as possessing few attractions. Clitheroe's heart sunk within him; and it sank deeper and deeper as it began to dawn upon him that the Hebrew had no wish to possess the garment, and, if he did so, he did so only to oblige the Christian youth. A bargain was at last struck; Paul departed with five dollars in his pocket—his dress-coat was a thing of the past.

What could he do next to extricate himself from his dubious dilemma? He had a small gold watch, a precious souvenir: "Gold is gold" said he, "and worth its weight in gold." He had the address of one who was known far and wide as "Uncle." He had heard of persons of the highest respectability seeking this uncle when close pressed, and there finding temporary relief at the hands of one who is in some respects a good Samaritan in disguise. Paul found it absolutely impossible for him to enter the not unattractive front of this establishment but there was a "private entrance" in a small dark alley-way; so delicate is the consideration of an uncle whose business it is to nourish those in distress.

One night, it was late at night, Clitheroe stole guiltily in through the private entrance, and sought succor of his uncle: this was an unctuous uncle, who was as sympathetic and emotional as an undertaker. Paul exhibited his watch; not for worlds would he part with it forever; money he must have at once, and surely some good angel would come to his assistance before many days; this state of affairs could not exist much longer. Mine uncle examined the watch with kindly eyes; with a pathetic shake of his head, a pitiful lifting of his bushy eyebrows, a commiserating shrug of his fat shoulders, and a petulant pursing of his plump lips as much as to say, "Well, it is a pity, but we must make the best of it, you know"—he told Clitheroe he would advance him ten dollars on the watch. For this the boy was to pay one dollar per week, and in the end receive his watch, as good as new, for the sum of ten dollars, as originally advanced. Paul hesitated, but consented since he had no choice in the matter.

"What name?" asked the Uncle, benevolently.

"P. Clitheroe," said Paul under his breath, as if he feared the whole world might know of his disgrace; he looked upon this transaction as nothing short of disgrace, and he wished to keep it a profound secret.

"Oh, yes; I know the name very well. Well, Mr. Clitheroe, here is your ticket; take good care of it; and here is your money—you will always pay your money in advance, and weekly, until you redeem your pledge. I deduct the dollar for the first week."

Clitheroe took the proffered money, and withdrew. To his surprise and chagrin he found himself possessed of but nine dollars. "It will not go far" thought he with a heavy sigh; "and where is the dollar to come from? I don't see that I have gained much by this exchange."

What he gained was this; for fifteen weeks he managed by the strictest economy to pay his dollar. At the end of that time, he no longer found it possible to even pay a dollar and the affair with the Uncle ended with his having lost, not only his watch, but sixteen dollars into the bargain.

A MONTH HAS PASSED: THE sun is streaming through the tall narrow windows of a small chapel; the air is flooded with the music that floats from the organ loft, the solemn strains of a requiem chanted by sweet boy-voices; clouds of fragrant incense half obscure the altar, where the priest in black vestments is offering the solemn sacrifice of the Mass for the repose of the soul of one whom Paul had loved dearly ever since he was a child. There is one chief mourner kneeling before the altar—it is Paul Clitheroe.

When Mass is over, while the exquisite silence of the place is broken only by the occasional note of some bird lodging in the branches of the trees without, Paul lingers in profound meditation. He is not at all the Paul whom we knew but a few months ago; through some mysterious influence he seems to have cast off his careless youth, and to have become a grave and thoughtful man.

From the chapel he wanders into the quiet library on the opposite side of a cloister, where the flowers grow in tangle, and a fountain splashes musically night and day, and the birds build and the bees swarm among the blossoms. Now we see him chatting with the Fathers as they stroll up and down in the sunshine; now musing over the graves of the Franciscan Friars who founded the early missions on the Coast; now dreaming in the ruins of the orchard—wandering always apart from the novices and the scholastics, who sometimes regard him curiously as if he were not wholly human but a kind of shadow haunting the place.

His heart grew warm and mellow as he sat by the adobe wall under the red-baked Spanish tiles, richly mossed with age, and contemplated the statue of the Madonna in the trellised shrine overgrown with passion flowers. There were votive offerings of flowers at her feet, and he laid his tribute there from day to day. Neither did he neglect to pay his visit to the shrine of St. Joseph, in the cloister, or St. Anthony of Padua, whom he loved best of all, and whose statue stood under the willows by the great pool of gold fish.

He used to count the hours and the quarter hours as they chimed in the belfry and he was beginning to grow fond of the inexorable routine and to find it passing sweet and restful.

He was unconsciously falling into a mode of life such as he had never known before, and he seemed to feel a growing repugnance to the world without him; how very far away it seemed now! He realized an increasing sense of security so long as he lodged within those gates. His dark robed companions, the amiable Fathers, cheered him, comforted him, strengthened him; and yet when his ghostly father one day sent word to Clitheroe that he desired to see him immediately, and thereupon insisted that the heart-broken boy accompany him to the retreat of his Order, he had no thought other than to offer Paul the change of scene which alone might help to tide the youth over the first crushing pangs of bereavement.

"Give me a week or two of your time," pleaded the good priest—"and I will introduce you to a course of life such as you have never known; it should interest and perhaps benefit you; possibly you may find it delightful. At any rate you must be hastened out of the morbid mood which now possesses you, even if we have to drag you by force."

So Paul went with him, suddenly and in a kind of desperation: his visit was prolonged from day to day, until some weeks had passed. Peace was returning to him—peace such as he had never known before.

Meanwhile certain of the young poet's friends had called to see him at the Eyrie, and to their amazement found his rooms deserted;

in the staring bay window with the inner blinds thrown wide open was notice "To Let." His landlady knew nothing of his whereabouts. He had said good bye to no one. His disappearance was perhaps the most mysterious of mysterious disappearances!

BOOK SECOND

Miss Juno

I

Miss Juno

There was an episode in the life of Paul Clitheroe, as yet unreferred to, that may perhaps throw some little light upon the mystery of his taking off; and in connection with this matter it is perhaps worth detailing.

One morning Paul found a drop-letter in the mail which greeted him daily. It ran as follows:

Dear Old Boy:

Don't forget the reception tomorrow. Some one will be here whom I wish you to know.

Most affectionately,
Harry English

The "tomorrow" referred to was the very day on which Paul received the sweet reminder. The reception of the message somewhat disturbed his customary routine. To be sure, he glanced through the morning journal as usual; repaired to the Greek chop-house with the dingy green walls, the smoked ceiling, the glass partition that separated the guests from a kitchen lined with shining copper pans, where a cook in a white paper cap wafted himself about in clouds of vapor, lit by occasional flashes of light and ever curling flames, like a soul expiating its sins in a prescribed but savory purgatory. He sat in his chosen seat, ignored his neighbors with his customary non-chalance, and returned to his room, as if nothing were about to happen. But he accomplished little, for he felt that the day was not wholly his; so slight a cause seemed to change the whole current of his life from hour to hour.

In due season Paul entered a street car which ran to the extreme limit of the city. Harry English lived not far from the terminus, and to the cozy home of this most genial and hospitable gentleman, the youth wended his way. The house stood upon the steep slope of a hill; the parlor was upon a level with the street,—a basement dining-room below it—but the rear of the house was quite in the air and all of the rear windows commanded a magnificent view of the North Bay with its Islands and the opposite mountainous shore.

"Infinite riches in a little room," was the expression which came involuntarily to Paul's lips the first time he crossed the threshold of Thespian Lodge. He might have said it of the Lodge any day in the week; the atmosphere was always balmy and soothing; one could sit there without talking or caring to talk; even without realizing that one was not talking and not being talked to; the silence was never ominous; it was a wholesome and restful home, where Paul was ever welcome and whither he often fled for refreshment.

The walls of the whole house were crowded with pictures, framed photographs and autographs, chiefly of theatrical celebrities; both "Harry," as the world familiarly called him, and his wife, were members of the dramatic profession and in their time had played many parts in almost as many lands and latitudes.

There was one chamber in this delightful home devoted exclusively to the delights of entomology and there the head of the house passed most of the hours which he was free to spend apart from the duties of his profession. He was a man of inexhaustible resources, consummate energy, and unflagging industry, yet one who was never in the least hurried or flurried; and he was Paul's truest and most judicious friend.

The small parlor at the English's was nearly filled with guests, when Paul Clitheroe arrived upon the scene. These guests were not sitting against the wall talking at each other; the room looked as if it were set for a scene in a modern Society comedy. In the bay-window, a bower of verdure, an extremely slender and diminutive lady was discoursing eloquently with the superabundant gesticulation of the successful society amateur; she was dilating upon the latest production of a minor poet whose bubble reputation was at that moment resplendent with local rainbows. Her chief listener was a languid beauty of literary aspirations, who, in a striking pose, was fit audience for the little lady as she frothed over with delightful, if not contagious enthusiasm.

Mrs. English, who had been a famous Belle—no one who knew her now would for a moment question the fact—devoted herself to the entertainment of a group of silent people, people of the sort that are not only colorless, but seem to dissipate the color in their immediate vicinity. The world is full of such; they spring up, unaccountably, in locations where they appear to the least advantage. Many a clever person who would delight to adorn a circle he longs to enter, and where he would be hailed with joy, through modesty, hesitates to enter it; while others who are of no avail in any wise whatever, walk bravely in and find themselves secure through a quiet system of polite insistence. Among the latter, the kind of people to be merely tolerated, we find, also, the large majority.

Two children remarkably self-possessed seized upon Paul the moment he entered the room; a beautiful lad as gentle and as graceful as a girl, and his tiny sister who bore herself with the dignity of a little lady of Lilliput. He was happy with them, quite as happy as if they were as old and experienced as their elders and as well entertained by them, likewise. He never in his life made the mistake that is, alas, made by most parents and guardians, of treating children as if they were little simpletons who can be easily deceived. How often they look with scorn upon their elders who are playing the hypocrite to eyes which are, for the most part, singularly critical! Having paid his respects to all present— he was known to all—Paul was led a willing captive into the chamber where Harry English and a brother professional, an eccentric comedian, who apparently never uttered a line which he had not learned out of a playbook, were examining with genuine enthusiasm certain cases of brilliantly tinted butterflies.

The children were quite at their ease in this house, and no wonder; California children are born philosophers; to them the marvels of the somewhat celebrated entomological collection were quite familiar; again and again they had studied the peculiarities of the most rare and beautiful specimens of insect life under the loving tutelage of their friend, who had spent his life and a small fortune in gathering together his treasures, and they were even able to explain in the prettiest fashion the origin and use of the many curious objects that were distributed about the rooms.

Meanwhile Mme. Lillian, the dramatic one, had left her bower in the bay window and was flitting to and fro in nervous delight; she had much to say and it was always worth listening to. With available opportunities she would have long since become famous and probably a leader of her sex; but it was her fate to coach those of meaner capacities who were ultimately to win fame and fortune while she toiled on, in genteel poverty, to the end of her weary days.

No two women could be more unlike than this many-summered butterfly, as she hovered among her friends, and the comedy queen who was still posing and making a picture of herself; the latter was regarded by the Society-privates, who haunted with fearful delight the receptions at Thespian Lodge, with the awe that inspired so many inexperienced people who look upon members of the dramatic profession as creatures of another and not a better world, and considerably lower than the angels.

Two hours passed swiftly by; nothing ever jarred upon the guests in this house; the perfect suavity of the host and hostess forbade anything like antagonism among their friends; and though such dissimilar elements might never again harmonize, they were tranquil for the time at least.

The adieus were being said in the chamber of entomology, which was somewhat over-crowded and faintly impregnated with the odor of *corrosive sublimate.* From the windows overlooking the bay there was visible the expanse of purple water and the tawny, sunburnt hills beyond, while pale-blue misty mountains marked the horizon with an undulating outline. A ship under full sail—a glorious and inspiring sight, was bearing down before the stiff breeze.

Mme. Lillian made an apt quotation which terminated with a Delsartean gesture and a rising inflection that seemed to exact something from somebody; the comedienne struck one of her property attitudes, so irresistibly comic that every one applauded, and Mme. Lillian laughed herself to tears; then they all drifted toward the door. As mankind in general has much of the sheep in him, one guest having got as far as the threshold the others followed; Paul was left alone with the Englishes and those clever youngsters, whose coachman, accustomed to waiting indefinitely at the Lodge, was dutifully dozing on the box seat. The children began to romp immediately upon the departure of the last guest, and during the riotous half hour that succeeded, there was a fresh arrival. The door-bell rang; Mrs. English, who chanced to be close at hand, turned to answer it and at once bubbled over with unaffected delight. Harry, still having his defunct legions in solemn review, recognized a cheery, un-American voice, and cried, "There she is at last!" as he hastened to meet the new-comer.

Paul was called to the parlor where a young lady of the ultra-blonde type stood with a faultlessly gloved hand in the hand of each of her friends; she was radiant with life and health. Of all the young ladies Paul could at that moment remember having seen, she was the most exquisitely clad; the folds of her gown fell about her form like the drapery of a statue; he was fascinated from the first moment of their

CHARLES WARREN STODDARD

meeting. He noticed that nothing about her was ever disarranged; neither was there anything superfluous or artificial, in manner or dress. She was in his opinion an entirely artistic creation. She met him with a perfectly frank smile, as if she were an old friend suddenly discovering herself to him, and when Harry English had placed the hand of this delightful person in one of Paul's she at once withdrew the other, which Mrs. English fondly held, and struck it in a hearty half-boyish manner upon their clasped hands, saying, "Awfully glad to see you Paul!" and she evidently meant it.

This was Miss Juno, an American girl bred in Europe, now, after years of absence, passing a season in her native land. Her parents, who had taken a country-home in one of the California Valleys, found in their only child all that was desirable in life. This was not to be wondered at; it may be said of her in the theatrical parlance that she "filled the stage." When Miss Juno dawned upon the scene the children grew grave and after a little delay, having taken formal leave of the company, they entered their carriage and were rapidly driven homeward.

If Paul and Miss Juno had been formed for one another and were now, at the right moment and under the most favorable auspices, brought together for the first time, they could not have mated more naturally. If Miss Juno had been a young man, instead of a very charming woman, she would of course have been Paul's chum. If Paul had been a young woman—some of his friends thought he had narrowly escaped it and did not hesitate to say so—he would instinctively have become her confidante. As it was, they promptly entered into a sympathetic friendship which seemed to have been without beginning and was apparently to be without end.

They began to talk of the same things at the same moment, often uttering the very same words, and then turned to one another with little shouts of unembarrassed laughter. They agreed upon all points, and aroused each other to a ridiculous pitch of enthusiasm over nothing in particular.

Harry English beamed; there was evidently nothing wanted to complete his happiness. Mrs. English, her eyes fairly dancing with delight, could only exclaim at intervals "Bless the boy," or "What a pair of children," then fondly pass her arm about the waist of Miss Juno— which was not waspish in girth—or rest her hand upon Paul's shoulder with a show of maternal affection peculiarly grateful to him. It was with difficulty the half-dazed young fellow could keep apart from Miss Juno.

If he found she had wandered into the next room, while he was engaged for a moment, he followed at his earliest convenience, and when their eyes met they smiled responsively without knowing why, and indeed not caring in the least to know.

They were as ingenuous as two children in their liking for one another; their trust in each other would have done credit to the Babes in the Wood. What Paul realized without any preliminary analysis of his mind or heart, was that he wanted to be near her, very near her; and that he was miserable when this was not the case. If she was out of his sight for a moment the virtue seemed to have gone out of him and he fell into the pathetic melancholy which he enjoyed in the days when he wrote a great deal of indifferent verse, and was burdened with the conviction that his mission in life was to make rhymes without end.

In those days, he had acquired the habit of pitying himself. The emotional middle-aged woman is apt to encourage the romantic young man in pitying himself; it is a grewsome habit, and stands sturdily in the way of all manly effort. Paul had outgrown it to a degree, but there is nothing easier in life than a relapse—perhaps nothing so natural, yet often so unexpected.

Too soon the friends who had driven Miss Juno to Thespian Lodge and passed on—being unacquainted with the Englishes—called to carry her away with them. She was shortly—in a day or two in fact—to rejoin her parents, and she did not hesitate to invite Paul to pay them a visit. This he assured her he would do with pleasure, and secretly vowed that nothing on earth should prevent him. They shook hands cordially at parting, and were still smiling their baby smiles in each other's faces when they did it. Paul leaned against the door-jamb, while the genial Harry and his wife followed his new-found friend to the carriage, where they were duly presented to its occupants—said occupants promising to place Thespian Lodge upon their list. As the carriage whirled away, Miss Juno waved that exquisitely gloved hand from the window and Paul's heart beat high; somehow he felt as if he had never been quite so happy. And this going away struck him as being a rather cruel piece of business. To tell the whole truth, he couldn't understand why she should go at all.

He felt it more and more, as he sat at dinner with his old friends, the Englishes, and ate, with less relish than common, the delicious Yorkshire pudding, and drank the musty ale. He felt it as he accompanied his friends to the theatre, where he sat with Mrs. English, while she watched with pride the husband whose impersonations she was never weary of witnessing; but Paul seemed to see him without recognizing him, and even the familiar voice sounded unfamiliar, or like a voice in a dream. He felt it more and more when good Mrs. English gave him a nudge toward the end of the evening and called him "a stupid," half in sport and half in earnest; and when he had delivered that excellent woman into the care of her liege-lord and had seen them securely packed into the horse-car that was to drag them tediously homeward in company with a great multitude of suffocating fellow-sufferers, he felt it; and all the way out the dark street and up the hill that ran, or seemed to run into outer darkness—where his home was—he felt as if he had never been the man he was until now, and that it was all for *her* sake and through *her* influence that this sudden and unexpected transformation had come to pass. And it seemed to him that if he were not to see her again, very soon, his life would be rendered valueless; and that only to see her were worth all the honor and glory that he had ever aspired to in his wildest dreams; and that to be near her always and to feel that he were much—nay everything—to her, as before God he felt that at that moment she was to him, would make his life one long Elysium, and to death would add a thousand stings.

II

In a Rose Garden

S aadi had no hand in it, yet all Persia could not outdo it. The whole valley ran to roses. They covered the earth; they fell from lofty trellises in fragrant cataracts; they played over the rustic arbors like fountains of color and perfume; they clambered to the cottage roof and scattered their bright petals in showers upon the grass. They were of every tint and texture; of high and low degree, modest or haughty as the case might be—but roses all of them, and such roses as California alone can boast. And some were fat or passe, and more's the pity, but all were fragrant, and the name of that sweet vale was Santa Rosa.

Paul was in the garden with Miss Juno. He had followed her thither with what speed he dared. She had expected him; there was not breathing-space for conventionality between these two. In one part of the garden sat an artist at his easel; by his side a lady somewhat his senior, but of the type of face and figure that never really grows old, or looks it. She was embroidering flowers from nature, tinting them to the life, and rivaling her companion in artistic effects. These were the parents of Miss Juno—or rather not quite that. Her mother had been twice married; first, a marriage of convenience darkened the earlier years of her life; Miss Juno was the only reward for an age of domestic misery. A clergyman joined these parties—God had nothing to do with the compact; it would seem that he seldom has. A separation very naturally and very properly followed in the course of time; a young child was the only possible excuse for the delay of the divorce. Thus are the sins of the fathers visited upon the grandchildren. Then came a marriage of love. The artist who had found his ideal had never known a moment's weariness, save when he was parted from her side. Their union was perfect; God had joined them. The stepfather to Miss Juno had always been like a big brother to her—even as her mother had always seemed like an elder sister.

Oh, what a trio was that, my countrymen, where liberty, fraternity and equality joined hands without howling about it and making themselves a nuisance in the nostrils of their neighbors.

Miss Juno stood in a rose-arbor and pointed to the artists at their work.

"Did you ever see anything like that, Paul?" said she.

"Like what?"

"Like those sweet simpletons yonder. They have for years been quite oblivious of the world about them. Thrones might topple, Empires rise and fall, it would matter nothing to them so long as their garden bloomed, and the birds nested and sung, and he sold a picture once in an age that the larder might not go bare."

"I've seen something like it, Miss Juno. I've seen fellows who never bothered themselves about the affairs of others,—who, in short minded their own business strictly—and they got credit for being selfish.

"Were they happy?"

"Yes, in their way. Probably their way wasn't my way, and their kind of happiness would bore me to death. You know happiness really can't be passed around, like bon-bons or sherbet, for everyone to taste. I hate bon-bons: do you like them?"

"That depends upon the quality and flavor—and—perhaps upon who offers them. I never buy bon-bons for my private and personal pleasure. Do any of you fellows really care for bon-bons?"

"That depends upon the kind of happiness we are in quest of; I mean the quality and flavor of the girl we are going to give them to."

"Have girls a flavor?"

"Some of them have—perhaps most of them haven't; neither have they form nor features, nor tint nor texture, nor anything that appeals to a fellow of taste and sentiment."

"I'm sorry for these girls of yours—"

"You needn't be sorry for the girls; they are not my girls, and not one of them ever will be mine if I can help it—"

"Oh, indeed!"

"They are nothing to me, and I'm nothing to them; but they are just— they are just the formless sort of thing that a formless sort of fellow always marries; they help to fill up the world, you know."

"Yes, they help to fill a world that is over full already. Poor Mama and Eugene don't know how full it is. When Gene wants to sell a picture and can't, he thinks it's a desert island."

"Probably they could live on a desert island and be perfectly happy and content," said Paul.

"Of course they could; the only trouble would be that unless some one called them at the proper hours they'd forget to eat—and some day they'd be found dead locked in their last embrace."

"How jolly!"

"Oh, very jolly for very young lovers; they are usually such fools!"

And yet, I believe I'd like to be a fool for love's sake, Miss Juno."

"Oh, Paul you are one for your own,—at least I'll think so, if you work yourself into this silly vein!"

Paul was silent and thoughtful. After a pause she continued.

"The trouble with you is, you fancy yourself in love with every new girl you meet—at least with the latest one, if she is in the least out of the ordinary line."

"The trouble with me is that I don't keep on loving the same girl long enough to come to the happy climax—if the climax *is* to be a happy one; of course it doesn't follow that it is to be anything of the sort. I've been brought up in the bosom of too many families to believe in the lasting quality of love. Yet they are happy, you say, those two gentle people perpetuating spring on canvas and cambric. See, there is a small cloud of butterflies hovering about them—one of them is panting in fairy-like ecstasy on the poppy that decorates your Mama's hat!"

Paul rolled a cigarette and offered it to Miss Juno, in a mild spirit of bravado. To his delight she accepted it, as if it were the most natural thing in the world for a girl to do. He rolled another and they sat down together in the arbor full of contentment.

"Have you never been in love?" asked Paul suddenly.

"Yes, I suppose so. I was engaged once; you know girls instinctively engage themselves to some one whom they fancy; they imagine themselves in love, and it is a pleasant fallacy. My engagement might have gone on forever, if he had contented himself with a mere engagement. He was a young army officer stationed miles and miles away. We wrote volumes of letters to each other—and they were clever letters; it was rather like a seaside novelette, our love affair. He was lonely, or restless, or something, and pressed his case. Then Mama and Gene—those ideal lovers—put their feet down and would none of it."

"And you—?"

"Of course I felt perfectly wretched for a whole week; and imagined myself cruelly abused. You see he was a foreigner, without money; he was heir to a title, but that would have brought him no advantages in the household."

"You recovered. What became of him?"

"I never learned. He seemed to fade away into thin air. I fear I was not very much in love."

"I wonder if all girls are like you—if they forget so easily?"

"You have yourself declared, that the majority have neither form nor feature; perhaps they have no feeling. How do men feel about a broken engagement?"

"I can only speak for myself. There was a time when I felt that marriage was the inevitable fate of all respectable people. Some one wanted me to marry a certain some one else. I didn't seem to care much about it; but my friend was one of those natural-born match-makers; she talked the young lady up to me in such a shape that I almost fancied myself in love and actually began to feel that I'd be doing her an injustice if I permitted her to go on loving and longing for the rest of her days. So one day I wrote her a proposal; it was the kind of proposal one might decline without injuring a fellow's feelings in the least—and she did it!" After a thoughtful pause he continued:

"By Jove. But wasn't I immensely relieved when her letter came; such a nice, dear good letter it was too, in which she assured me there had evidently been a mistake somewhere, and nothing had been further from her thoughts than the hope of marrying me. So she let me down most beautifully—"

"And offered to be a sister to you?"

"Perhaps; I don't remember now; I always felt embarrassed after that, when her name was mentioned. I couldn't help thinking what an infernal ass I'd made of myself."

"It was all the fault of your friend."

"Of course it was; I'd never have dreamed of proposing to her, if I hadn't been put up to it by the match-maker. O, what a lot of miserable marriages are brought on in just this way! You see when I like a girl ever so much, I seem to like her too well to marry her. I think it would be mean of me to marry her."

"Why?"

"Because—because I'd get tired after a while; everybody does, sooner or later;—everybody save your Mama and Eugene—and then I'd say something or do something I ought not to say or do, and I'd hate myself for it; or she'd say something or do something that would make me hate her. We might, of course, get over it and be very nice to one another; but we could never be quite the same again. Wounds leave scars, and you can't forget a scar—can you?"

"You may scar too easily!"

"I suppose I do, and that is the very best reason why I should avoid the occasion of one."

"So you have resolved never to marry?"

"O, I've resolved it a thousand times, and yet, somehow I'm forever meeting some one a little out of the common; some one who takes me by storm, as it were; some one who seems to me a kind of revelation, and then I feel as if I must marry her whether or no; sometimes I fear I shall wake up and find myself married in spite of myself—wouldn't that be frightful?"

"Frightful indeed—and then you'd have to get used to it, just as most married people get used to it in the course of time. You know it's a very matter of fact world we live in, and it takes very matter of fact people to keep it in good running order."

"Yes. But for these drudges, these hewers of wood and drawers of water, that ideal pair over yonder could not go on painting and embroidering things of beauty with nothing but the butterflies to bother them."

"Butterflies don't bother; they open new vistas of beauty, and they set examples that it would do the world good to follow; the butterfly says, 'my mission is to be brilliant and jolly and to take no thought of the morrow.'"

"It's the thought of the morrow, Miss Juno, that spoils today for me—that morrow—who is going to pay the rent of it? Who is going to keep it in food and clothes?"

"Paul, you have already lived and loved, where there is no rent to pay and where the clothing worn is not worth mentioning; as for the food and the drink in that delectable land, nature provides them both. I don't see why you need to take thought of the morrow; all you have to do is to take passage for some South Sea Island, and let the world go by."

"But the price of the ticket, my friend; where is that to come from? To be sure I'm only a bachelor, and have none but myself to consider. Good heavens! What would I do if I had a wife and family to provide for?"

"You'd do as most other fellows in the same predicament do; you'd provide for them as well as you could; and if that wasn't sufficient you'd desert them, or blow your brains out and leave them to provide for themselves."

"An old bachelor is a rather comfortable old party. I'm satisfied with my manifest destiny; but I'm rather sorry for old maids—aren't you?"

"That depends; of course everything in life depends; some of the most beautiful, the most blessed, the most bountifully happy women I have ever known were old maids; I propose to be one myself—if I live long enough!"

After an interlude, during which the bees boomed among the honey-blossoms, the birds caroled on the boughs, and the two artists laughed softly as they chatted at their delightful work, Paul resumed—

"Do you know, Miss Juno, this anti-climax strikes me as being exceedingly funny? When I met you the other day, I felt as if I'd met my fate. I know well enough that I'd felt that way often before, and promptly recovered from the attack. I certainly never felt it in the same degree until I came face to face with you. I was never quite so fairly and squarely face to face with any one before. I came here because I could not help myself. I simply had to come, and to come at once. I was resolved to propose to you and to marry you without a cent, if you'd let me. I didn't expect that you'd let me, but I felt it my duty to find out. I'm dead sure that I was very much in love with you—and I am now; but somehow it isn't that spoony sort of love that makes a man unwholesome and sometimes drives him to drink or to suicide. I suppose I love you too well to want to marry you; but God knows how glad I am that we have met, and I hope that we shall never really part again."

"Paul!"—Miss Juno's rather too pallid cheeks were slightly tinged with rose; she seemed more than ever to belong to that fair garden, to have become a part of it, in fact;—"Paul" said she, earnestly enough, "you're an awfully good fellow, and I like you *so* much; I shall always like you; but if you had been fool enough to propose to me I should have despised you. Shake!" And she extended a most shapely hand that clasped his warmly and firmly. While he still held it without restraint he added:

"Why I like you so much is because you are unlike other girls; that is to say, you're perfectly natural."

"Most people who think me unlike other girls, think me unnatural for that reason. It is hard to be natural, isn't it?"

"Why, no, I think it is the easiest thing in the world to be natural. I'm as natural as I can be, or as anybody can be."

"And yet I've heard you pronounced a bundle of affectations."

"I know that—it's been said in my hearing, but I don't care in the least; it is natural for the perfectly natural person *not* to care in the least."

"I think, perhaps, it is easier for boys to be natural, than for girls," said Miss Juno.

"Yes, boys are naturally more natural," replied Paul with much confidence.

Miss Juno smiled an amused smile.

Paul resumed—"I hardly ever knew a girl who didn't wish herself a boy. Did you ever see a boy who wanted to be a girl?"

"I've seen some who ought to have been girls—and who would have made very droll girls. I know an old gentleman who used to bewail the degeneracy of the age and exclaim in despair, 'Boys will be girls!'" laughed Miss Juno.

"Horrible thought! But why is it that girl-boys are so unpleasant while tom-boys are delightful?"

"I don't know," replied she, "unless the girl-boy has lost the charm of his sex, that is manliness; and the tom-boy has lost the defect of hers—a kind of selfish dependence."

"I'm sure the girls like you, don't they?" he added.

"Not always; and there are lots of girls I can't endure!"

"I've noticed that women who are most admired by women are seldom popular with men; and that the women the men go wild over are little appreciated by their own sex," said Paul.

"Yes, I've noticed that; as for myself my best friends are masculine; but when I was away at boarding-school my chum, who was immensely popular, used to call me Jack!"

"How awfully jolly; may I call you 'Jack' and will you be my chum?"

"Of course I will; but what idiots the world would think us."

"Who cares?" cried he defiantly, "there are millions of fellows this very moment who would give their all for such a pal as you are—Jack!"

There was a fluttering among the butterflies; the artists had risen and were standing waist-deep in the garden of gracious things; they were coming to Paul and Miss Juno, and in amusing pantomime announcing that pangs of hunger were compelling their return to the cottage; the truth is, it was long past the lunch hour—and a large music-box which had been set in motion when the light repast was laid—had failed to catch the ear with its tinkling aria.

All four of the occupants of the garden turned leisurely toward the cottage. Miss Juno had rested her hand on Paul's shoulder and said in a delightfully confidential way: "Let it be a secret that we are chums, dear boy—the world is such an idiot."

"All right, Jack," whispered Paul, trying to hug himself in delight, 'Little secrets are cozy.'"

And in the scent of the roses it was duly embalmed.

CHARLES WARREN STODDARD

III

Where the Bee Sucks

Happy is the man who is without encumbrances—that is if he knows how to be happy. Whenever Paul Clitheroe found the burden of the day becoming oppressive he cast it off, and sought solace in a change of scene. He could always, or almost always, do this at a moment's notice. It chanced, upon a certain occasion, when a little community of artists were celebrating the sale of a great picture—the masterpiece of one of their number—that word was sent to Paul to join their feast. He found the large studio where several of them worked intermittently, highly decorated; a table was spread in a manner to have awakened an appetite even upon the palate of the surfeited; there were music and dancing, and bacchanalian revels that went on and on from night to day and on to night again. It was a veritable feast of lanterns, and not until the last one had burned to the socket and the wine-vats were empty and the studio strewn with unrecognizable debris and permeated with odors stale, flat and unprofitable, did the revels cease. Paul came to dine; he remained three days; he had not yet worn out his welcome, but he had resolved, as was his wont at intervals, to withdraw from the world, and so he returned to the Eyrie,—which was ever his initial step toward the accomplishment of the longed for end.

Directly after the Foxlair episode, mentioned in Book I, Paul received the breeziest of letters; it was one of a series of racy rhapsodies that came to him bearing the Santa Rosa postmark. They were such letters as a fellow might write to a college chum, but with no line that could have brought a blush to the cheek of modesty—not that the college chum is necessarily given to the inditing of such epistles. These letters were signed "Jack."

"Jack" wrote to say how the world was all in bloom and the rose garden one bewildering maze of blossoms; how Mama was still embroidering from nature in the midst thereof, crowned with a wreath of butterflies and with one uncommonly large one perched upon her Psyche shoulder and fanning her cheek with its brilliantly dyed wing; how Eugene was revelling in his art, painting lovely pictures of the old Spanish Missions with shadowy outlines of the ghostly fathers, long since departed, haunting the dismantled cloisters; how the air was like the breath of Heaven, and the twilight unspeakably pathetic, and they were all three constantly reminded of Italy and forever talking of Rome and the Campagna, and Venice, and imagining themselves at home again and Paul with them, for they had resolved that he was quite out of his element in California; they had sworn he must be rescued; he must return with them to Italy and that right early. He must wind up his affairs and set his house in order at once and forever; he should never go back to it again, but live a new life and a gentler life in that oldest and most gentle of lands; they simply *must* take him with them and seat him by the shore of the Venetian Sea, where he could enjoy his melancholy, if he must be melancholy, and find himself for the first time provided with a suitable background. This letter came to him inlaid with rose petals; they showered upon him in all their fragrance as he read the inspiring pages, and, since "Jack" with quite a martial air had issued a mandate which ran as follows, "Order No. 19—Paul Clitheroe, will, upon receipt of this, report immediately at headquarters at Santa Rosa," he placed the key of his outer door in his pocket and straightway departed without more ado.

THEY SWUNG IN INDIVIDUAL HAMMOCKS, Paul and "Jack," within the rose-screened veranda. The conjugal affinities, Violet and Eugene, were lost to the world in the depths of the rose-garden beyond sight and hearing.

Said Jack, resuming a rambling conversation which had been interrupted by the noisy passage of a bee, "That particular bee, reminds me of some people who fret over their work, and who make others who are seeking rest, extremely uncomfortable."

Paul was thoughtful for a few moments and then remarked: "And yet it is a pleasant work he is engaged in, and his days are passed in the fairest fields; he evidently enjoys his trade even if he does seem to bustle about it. I can excuse the buzz and the hum in him, when I can't always in the human tribes."

"If you knew what he was saying just now, perhaps you'd find him as disagreeable as the man who is condemned to earn his bread in the sweat of his brow, and makes more or less of a row about it."

"Very likely, Jack, but these bees are born with business instincts, and they can't enjoy loafing; they don't know how to be idle. Being as busy as a busy bee must be being very busy!"

"There is the hum of the hive in that phrase, old boy! I'm sure you've been working up to it all along. Come now, confess, you've had that in hand for some little time."

"Well, what if I have? That is what writers do, and they have to do it. How else can they make their dialogue in the least attractive? Did you ever write a story, Jack?"

"No, of course not; how perfectly absurd!"

"Not in the least absurd. You've been reading novels ever since you were born. You've the knack of the thing, the telling of a story, the developing of a plot, the final wind-up of the whole concern, right at your tongue's end."

"Paul, you're an idiot."

"Idiot, Jack? I'm nothing of the sort and I can prove what I've just been saying to you about yourself. Now, listen and don't interrupt me until I've said my say."

Paul caught hold of a branch of vine close at hand and set his hammock swinging slowly. Miss Juno settled herself more comfortably in hers, and seemed much interested and amused.

"Now," said Paul, with a comical air of importance—"Now, any one who has anything at his tongue's end, has it, or *can*, just as well as not, have it at his finger's end. If you can tell a story well, and you can Jack, you know you can, you can write it just as well. You have only to tell it with your pen instead of with your lips; and if you will only write it exactly as you speak it, so long as your verbal version is a good one, your pen version is bound to be equally as good; moreover it seems to me that in this way one is likely to adopt the most natural style, which is, of course, the best of all styles. Now what do you say to that?"

"Oh, nothing," after a little pause—"however, I doubt that any one, male or female, can take up pen for the first time and tell a tale like a practiced writer."

"Of course not. The practiced writer has a style of his own, a conventional narrative style which may be very far from nature. People in books very seldom talk as they do in real life. When people in books begin to talk like human beings the reader thinks the dialogue either commonplace or mildly realistic, and votes it a bore."

"Then why try to write as one talks? Why not cultivate the conventional style of the practiced writer?"

"Why talk commonplace?" cried Paul a little tartly: "Of course most people must do so if they talk at all, and they are usually the people who talk all the time. But I have known people whose ordinary conversation was extraordinary, and worth putting down in a book—every word of it."

"In my experience," said Miss Juno, "people who talk like books are a burden."

"They needn't talk like the conventional book, I tell you. Let them have something to say and say it cleverly—that is the kind of conversation to make books of."

"What if all that we've been saying here, under the rose, as it were, were printed just as we've said it?"

"What if it were? It would at least be natural, and we've been saying something of interest to each other; why should it not interest a third party?"

Miss Juno smiled and rejoined, "I am not a confirmed eavesdropper, but I often find myself so situated that I cannot avoid overhearing what people are saying to one another; it is seldom that, under such circumstances, I hear anything that interests me."

"Yes, but if you knew the true story of those very people, all that they may be saying in your hearing would no doubt possess an interest, inasmuch as it would serve to develop their history."

"Our conversation is growing a little thin, Paul, don't you think so? We couldn't put all this into a book."

"If it helped to give a clue to our character and our motives, we could. The thing is to be interesting: if we are interesting, in ourselves, by reason of our original charm or our unconventionality, almost anything we might say or do ought to interest others. Conventional people are never interesting."

"Yet the majority of mankind is conventional to a degree; the conventionals help to fill up; their habitual love of conventionality, or their fear of the unconventional is what keeps them in their places. This is very fortunate. On the other hand, a world full of people too clever to be kept in their proper spheres, would be simply intolerable. But there is no danger of this!"

"Yes, you are right," said Paul after a moment's pause;—"you are interesting, and that is why I like you so well."

"You mean that I am unconventional?"

"Exactly. And, as I said before, that is why I'm so awfully fond of you. By Jove, I'm so glad I'm not in love with you, Jack."

"So am I, old boy; I couldn't put up with that at all; you'd have to go by the next train, you know; you would, really. And yet, if we are to write a novel apiece we shall be obliged to put love into it; love with a very large L."

"No we wouldn't; I'm sure we wouldn't."

Miss Juno shook her golden locks in doubt—Paul went on persistently:—"I'm dead sure we wouldn't; and to prove it some day I'll write a story without its pair of lovers; everybody shall be more or less spoony—but nobody shall be really in love."

"It wouldn't be a story, Paul."

"It would be a history, or a fragment of a history, a glimpse of a life at any rate, and that is as much as we ever get of the lives of those around us. Why can't I tell you the story of one fellow—of myself for example; how one day I met this person, and the next day I met that person, and next week some one else comes on to the stage, and struts his little hour and departs. I'm not trying to give my audience, my readers, any knowledge of that other fellow. My reader must see for himself how each of those fellows in his own way has influenced me. The story is my story, a study of myself, nothing more or less. If the reader don't like me he may lay me down in my cloth or paper cover, and have nothing more to do with me. If I'm not a hero, perhaps it's not so much my fault as my misfortune. That people are interested in me, and show it in a thousand different ways, assures me that *my* story, not the story of those with whom I'm thrown in contact, is what interests them. It's a narrow-gauge, single-track story, but it runs through a delightful bit of country, and if my reader wants to look out of my windows and see things as I see them and find out how they influence me, he is welcome; if he doesn't, he may get off at the very next station and change cars for Elsewhere."

"I shall have love in my story," said Miss Juno, with an amusing touch of sentiment that on her lips sounded like polite comedy.

"You may have all the love you like, and appeal to the same old novel reader who has been reading the same sort of love-story for the last hundred years, and when you've finished your work and your reader has stood by you to the sweet or bitter end, no one will be any wiser or better. You've taught nothing, you've untaught nothing—and there you are!"

"Oh! A young man with a mission! Do you propose to revolutionize?"

"No; revolutions only soil the water. You might as well try to make water flow up hill as to really revolutionize anything. I'd beautify the banks of the stream, and round the sharp turns in it, and weed it out, and sow water-lilies, and set the white swan with her snow-flecked breast afloat. That's what I'd do!"

"That's the art of the landscape gardener; I don't clearly see how it is of benefit to the novelist, Paul! Now, honestly, is it?"

"You don't catch my meaning, Jack; girls are deuced dull, you know,—I mean obtuse." Miss Juno flushed. "I wasn't referring to the novel; I was saying that instead of writing my all in a vain effort to revolutionize anything in particular, I'd try to get all the good I could out of the existing evil, and make the best of it. But let's not talk in this vein any longer; I hate argument. Argument is nothing but a logical or illogical set-to; begin it as politely as you please, it is not long before both parties throw aside their gloves and go in with naked and bloody fists; one of the two gets knocked out, but he hasn't been convinced of anything in particular; he was not in condition, that is all; better luck next time."

"Have you the tobacco, Paul?"—asked Miss Juno, extending her hand. The tobacco was silently passed from one hammock to the other; each rolled a cigarette, and lit it. Paul blew a great smoke ring into the air; his companion blew a lesser one that shot rapidly after the larger halo, and the two were speedily blended in a pretty vapor wraith.

"That's the ghost of an argument, Jack," said Paul glancing above. He resumed: "What I was about to say when I was interrupted"—this was his pet joke; he knew well enough that he had been monopolizing the conversation of the morning—"What I was about to say was this: My novel shall be full of love, but you won't know that it is love—I mean the every-day love of the every-day people. In my book everybody is going to love everybody else—or almost everybody else; if there is any sort of a misunderstanding it shan't matter much. I hate rows; I believe in the truest and the fondest fellowship. What is true love? It is bosom-friendship; that is the purest passion of love. It is the only love that lasts."

There was a silence for the space of some minutes; Paul and Miss Juno were quietly, dreamily, smoking. Without, among the roses, there was the boom of bees; the carol of birds, the flutter of balancing butterflies. Nature was very soothing, she was in one of her sweetest moods. The two friends were growing drowsy. Miss Juno, if she at times betrayed a feminine fondness for argument, was certainly in no haste to provoke Paul to a further discussion of the quality of love or friendship; presently she began rather languidly:

"You were saying I ought to write, and that you believe I can, if I will only try. I'm going to try; I've been thinking of something that happened within my knowledge; perhaps I can make a magazine sketch of it."

"Oh, please write it, Jack! Write it, and send the manuscript to me, that I may place it; will you? Promise me you will!" The boy was quite enthusiastic, and his undisguised pleasure in the prospect of seeing something from the pen of his *Pal*—as he loved to call Miss Juno— seemed to awaken a responsive echo in her heart.

"I will, Paul; I promise you!"—and the two struck hands on it.

IV

HONEY IN THE HONEYCOMB

When Paul returned to the Eyrie, it had been decided that Miss Juno was to at once begin her first contribution to periodic literature. She had found her plot; she had only to tell her story in her own way, just as if she were recounting it to Paul. Indeed, at his suggestion, she had promised to sit with pen in hand and address him as if he were actually present. In this way he hoped she would drop into the narrative style natural to her, and so attractive to her listeners.

As for Paul Clitheroe, he was to make inquiry among his editorial friends in the Misty City, and see if he might not effect some satisfactory arrangement with one or another of them, whereby he would be placed in a position enabling him to go abroad in the course of a few weeks, and remain abroad indefinitely. He would make Venice his headquarters; he would have the constant society of his friends; the fellowship of Jack; together, after the joint literary labors of the day, they would stem the sluggish tide of the darksome canals and exchange sentiment and cigarette-smoke in mutual delight. Paul was to write a weekly or a semi-monthly letter to the journal employing him as a special correspondent. At intervals, in the company of his friends, or alone, he would set forth upon one of those charming excursions so fruitful of picturesque experience, and return to his lodgings on the Schiavoni, to work them up into magazine articles; these would later of course get into book-form; from the book would come increased reputation, a larger source of revenue, and the contentment of success which he so longed for, so often thought he had found, and so seldom enjoyed for any length of time.

All this was to be arranged,—or rather the means to which all this was the delightful end—was to be settled as soon as possible. Miss Juno, having finished her story, was to send word to Paul and he was to hie him to the Rose Garden; thereafter at an ideal dinner, elaborated in honor of the occasion, Eugene was to read the maiden effort, while the author, sustained by the sympathetic presence of her admiring Mama and her devoted Paul, awaited the verdict.

This was to be the test—a trying one for Miss Juno. As for Paul he felt quite patriarchal and yet, so genuine and so deep was his interest in the future of his protege, that he was already showing symptoms of anxiety.

The article having been sent to the editor of the first magazine in the land, the family would be ready to fold its æsthetic tent and depart; Paul, of course, accompanying them.

It was a happy thought; visions of Venice; the moonlit lagoon; the reflected lamps plunging their tongues of flame into the sea; the humid air, the almost breathless silence, broken at intervals by the baying of deep-mouthed bells; the splash of oars; the soft tripping measure of human voices and the refrain of the Gondoliers; Jack by his side—Jack now in her element, with the maroon fez of the distinguished howadji tilted upon the back of her handsome head, her shapely finger-nails stained with henna, her wrists weighed down with their scores of tinkling bangles! Could anything be jollier?

Paul gave himself up to the full enjoyment of this dream. Already he seemed to have overcome every obstacle, and to be revelling in the subdued but sensuous joys of the Adriatic queen. Sometimes he had fled in spirit to the sweet seclusion of the cloisteral life at San Lazaro. Byron did it before him;—the plump, the soft-voiced, mild-visaged little Arminians will tell you all about that, and take immense pleasure in telling it. Paul had also known a fellow-writer who had emulated Byron, and had even distanced the Byron record in one respect at least— he had outstayed his Lordship at San Lazaro!

Sometimes Paul turned hermit, in imagination, and dwelt alone upon the long sands of the melancholy Lido; not seeing Jack, or anybody, save the waiter at the neighboring restaurant, for days and days together. It was immensely diverting, this dream-life that Paul led in far distant Venice. It was just the life he loved, the ideal life, and it wasn't costing him a cent—no not a *soldo*, to speak more in the Venetian manner.

While he was looking forward to the life to come, he had hardly time to perfect his arrangements for a realization of it. He was to pack everything and store it in a bonded warehouse, where it should remain until he had taken root abroad. Then he would send for it and settle in the spot he loved best of all, and there write and dream and drink the wine of the country, while the Angelus bells ringing thrice a day awoke him to a realizing sense of the fairy-like flight of time just as they have been doing for ages past, and, let us hope, as they will continue to do forever and forever.

One day he stopped dreaming of Italy, and resolved to secure his engagement as a correspondent. Miss Juno had written him that her sketch was nearly finished; that he must hold himself in readiness to answer her summons at a moment's notice. The season was advancing; no time was to be lost, etc. Paul started at once for the office of his favorite journal; his interview was not entirely satisfactory. Editors, one and all, as he called upon them in succession, didn't seem especially anxious to send the young man abroad for an indefinite period; the salary requested seemed exorbitant. They each made a proposition; each said: "This is the best I can do at present; go to the other offices, and if you receive a better offer we advise you to take it." This seemed reasonable enough, but as their best rate was fifteen dollars for one letter a week he feared that even the highly-respectable second-class accommodations of all sorts to which he must confine himself would be beyond his means.

Was he losing interest in the scheme which had afforded him so many hours of sweet, if not solid, satisfaction? No, not exactly. Poverty was more picturesque abroad than in his prosaic native land. His song was not quite so joyous, that was all; he would go to Italy; he would take a smaller room; he would eat at the Trattoria of the people; he would make studies of the peasant, the contadini. Jack had written, "There is pie in Venice when we are there; Mama knows how to make pie; pie cannot be purchased elsewhere. Love is the price thereof!" And pie is very filling. Yes, he would go to Europe on fifteen dollars per week and find paradise in the bright particular Venetian Pie!

V

A Mystery Half Unraveled

After many days the great change came as recorded in Book I. Everybody knew that Paul Clithroe had disappeared without so much as a "Good-by" to his most intimate friends. Curiosity was excited for a little while, but for a little while only. Soon he was forgotten, or remembered by no one save those who had known and loved him and who at intervals regretted him.

And Miss Juno? Ah, Miss Juno, the joy of Paul's young dreams! Having been launched successfully at his hands, and hoping in her brave, off-hand way to be of service to him, she continued to write as much for his sake as for her own; she knew it would please him beyond compare were she to achieve a pronounced literary success. He had urged her to write a novel. She had lightly laughed him to scorn—and had kept turning in her mind the possible plot for a tale. One day it suddenly took shape; the whole thing seemed to her perfectly plain sailing; if Clitheroe had launched her upon that venturesome sea, she had suddenly found herself equipped and able to sail without the aid of any one.

She had written to Paul of her joy in this new discovery. Before her loomed the misty outlines of fair far-islands; she was about to set forth to people these. Oh, the joy of that! The unspeakable joy of it! She spread all sail on this voyage of discovery—she asked for nothing more save the prayers of her old comrade. She longed to have him near her so that together they might discuss the situations in her story, one after another. If he were only in Venice they would meet daily over their dinner and after dinner she would read to him what she had had written since they last met; then they would go in a gondola for a moonlight cruise; of course it was always moonlight in Venice! Would this not be delightful and just as an all-wise Providence meant it should be? Paul had read something like this in the letters which she used to write him when he was divided against himself; when he began to feel himself sinking, without a hand to help him. Venice was out of the question then; it were vain for him to even dream of it.

So time went on; Miss Juno became a slave of the lamp; her work grew marvelously under her pen. Her little people led her a merry chase; they whispered in her ears night and day; she got no rest of them—but rose again and again to put down the clever things they said and so, almost before she knew it, her novel had grown into three fine English volumes with inch broad margins, half-inch spacings, large type and heavy paper. She was amazed to find how important her work had become.

Fortune favored her. She found a publisher who was ready to bring out her book at once; two sets of proofs were forwarded to her; these she corrected with deep delight, returning one to her London publisher and sending one to America, where another publisher was ready to issue the work simultaneously with the English print.

It made its appearance under a pseudonyme in England—anonymously in America. What curiosity it awakened may be judged by the instantaneous success of the work in both countries: Tauchnitz at once added it to his fascinating list; the French and German translators negotiated for the right to run it as a serial in Paris and Berlin journals. Considerable curiosity was awakened concerning the identity of the authorship and the personal paragraphers made a thousand conjectures all of which helped the sale of the novel immensely and amused Miss Juno and her confidants beyond expression.

All this was known to Clitheroe before he had reached the climax that forced him to the wall. He had written to Miss Juno; and he had called her "Jack" as of old, but he felt and she realized that he felt that the conditions were changed. The atmosphere of the rose garden was gone forever; the hopes and aspirations that were so easy and so airy then, had folded their wings like bruised butterflies, or faded like the flowers. She resolved to wait until he had recovered his senses and then perhaps he would come to Venice and to them—which, in her estimation amounted to one and the same thing.

She wrote to him no more; he had not written her for weeks; save only the few lines of congratulation on the success of her novel, and to thank her for the Author's copy she had sent him; the three-volume London edition with a fond inscription on the fly-leaf—a line in each volume. This was the end of all that.

Once more she wrote, but not to Clitheroe; she wrote to a friend she had known when she was in the far West, one who knew Paul well and was always eager for news of him.

The letter, or part of it, ran as follows:

Of course such weather as this is not to be shut out of doors; we feed on it; we drink it in; we bathe in it, body and soul. Ah my friend know a June in Venice before you die! Don't dare to die until you have become saturated with the aerial-aquatic beauty of this Divine Sea-City!

Oh, I was about to tell you something when the charms of this Syren made me half delirious and of course I forgot all else in life—I always do so. Well, as we leave in a few days for the delectable Dolamites we are making our rounds of P. R. C.'s; that is we are revisiting every nook and corner in the lagoon so dear to us. We invariably do this; it is the most delicious leave-taking imaginable. If I were only Niobe I'd water these shore with tears—I'm sure I would:—but you know I never weep; I never did; I don't know how; there is not a drop of brine in my whole composition.

Dear me how I do rattle on—but you know my moods and will make due allowance for what might strike the cold, unfeeling world as being garrulity.

We had resolved to visit that most enchanting of all Italian shrines, San Francisco del Deserto. We had not been there for an age; you know it is rather a long pull over, and one waits for the most perfect hour when one ventures upon the outskirts of the lagoon.

Oh, the unspeakable loveliness of that perfect day! The mellowing haze that veiled the water; the heavenly blue of the sea, a mirror of the sky, and floating in between the two, so that one could not be quite sure whether it slumbered in the lap of the sea or hung upon the bosom of the sky, that ideal summer island—San Francisco del Deserto.

You know it is only a few acres in extent—not more than six I fancy, and four-fifths of it are walled about with walls that stand knee-deep in sea-grasses. Along, and above it, are thrust the tapering tops of those highly decorative cypresses without which Italy would not be herself at all. There is such a monastery there—an ideal one, with cloister, and sun-dial, and marble-curbed well, and all that; at least so I am told; we poor feminine creatures are not permitted to cross the thresholds of these Holy Houses. This reminds me of a remark I heard made by a very clever woman who wished to have a glimpse of the interior of that impossible Monte Casino on the mountain top between Rome and Naples. Of course she was refused admission; she turned upon the poor Benedictine, who was only obeying orders—it is a rule of the house, you know—and said, "Why do you refuse me admission to this shrine? Is it because I am of the same sex as the mother of your God?" But she didn't get in for all that. Neither have I crossed the threshold of San Francisco del Deserto, but I have wandered upon the green in front of the little chapel; and sat under the trees in contemplation of the sea and wished—yes, really and truly wished—that I were a bare-footed Franciscan Friar with nothing to do but look picturesque in such an earthly paradise.

What do you think happened when we were there the other day? Now at last I am coming to it. We were all upon the Campo in front of the chapel—Violet, Eugene and I; the Angelus had just rung; it was the hour of all hours in one's life-time; the deepening twilight—we had the moon to light us on our homeward way—the inexpressible loveliness of the atmosphere, the unutterable peace, the unspeakable serenity—the repose in nature—I cannot begin to express myself!

Out of the chapel came the Father Superior. He knows us very well, for we have often visited the island; he always offers us some refreshments, a cup of mass wine, or a dish of fruit, and so he did on this occasion. We were in no hurry to leave the shore and so accepted his invitation to be seated under the trees while he ordered refreshments.

Presently he returned and was shortly followed by a young friar whom we had never seen before; there are not many of them there—a dozen perhaps—and their faces are more or less familiar to us, for even we poor women may kneel without the gratings in their little chapel and so we have learned to know the faces we have seen there in the choir. But this one was quite new to us and so striking; his eyes were never raised; he offered us a dish of bread and olives, while the Abbot poured our wine, and the very moment we had served ourselves he quietly withdrew.

I could think of but one thing—indeed we all thought of it at the same moment—'tis Browning's—

> "What's become of Waring
> Since he gave us all the slip?"

You know the lines well enough. Why did we think of it?—because we were all startled, so startled that the abbot who usually sees us to our gondola, made his abrupt adieus, on some slight pretext, and the door of the monastery was bolted fast.

CHARLES WARREN STODDARD

Oh me! How long it takes to tell a little tale—to be sure! We knew that face, the face of the young friar; we knew the hand—it was unmistakeable; we have all agreed upon it and are ready to swear to it on our oaths! That novice was none other than Paul Clitheroe!

BOOK THIRD

Little Mama

I

A Mysterious Stranger

Doubtless Miss Juno was satisfied and happy in the belief that she had plucked out the heart of the mystery that hung over the disappearance of Paul Clitheroe. Her discovery at San Francisco del Deserto was accepted as proof positive that Paul, worn out with watching and waiting for the turn of the tide in his affairs that should lead on to fortune, had fled from the weary world and sought final refuge in the most picturesque and poetical of monasteries.

We are often deceived in faces, and even human forms. Masculine and feminine types are limited; one can almost count them on one's fingers. To confess the truth, Miss Juno was—was what? Well! We shall see. We shall see Paul Clitheroe and his struggles with the inevitable from another point of view, and therefore shall be better able to judge what course he would be most likely to take, when forbearance had ceased to be a virtue and it became necessary to take the final step.

Thus are we seen of men, each and all of us. The testimony of one who thinks he knows us; the testimony of another who knows he knows us—these testaments are discredited scornfully by a third who has known us all our lives. Pray who is right where none are infallible? Let us sift the last evidence in the case and draw to a conclusion.

The Foxlair affair was scarcely a nine day's wonder. How could it be? Such things are happening hourly. Paul, with his accustomed ease had forgiven all, and was thinking amiably of the pleasant times he had enjoyed with his late companion, the adventurer. Having resolved that fifteen dollars a week in advanced instalments, coupled with the artistic *pie* of Venice and the moral support of his delightful Jack was sufficient unto the day abroad, he was now wondering how all his bric-a-brac was to be bestowed and where the packing cases were to come from. This perplexing problem occupied a good many of his waking hours, and at intervals disturbed his slumbers.

Before anything was accomplished, he received a dispatch from the hands of a messenger-boy and was agreeably surprised to find that Laurella Laurel, a mountain poetess, not without pleasant reports from her native wild-wood, had come to town and desired his presence.

They had exchanged numerous letters of a very friendly character; had even addressed complimentary verse to one another; their several photographs had passed from hand to hand; but in all these symptoms of increasing familiarity there was nothing in the least compromising. They were the best of friends, that was all; and Paul was heartily glad of the opportunity of meeting "Laurella" of the romantic name and fame, face to face.

He hastened to her temporary lodgings, at as early an hour as was admissible. He sent up his card, and was at once admitted to a chamber, both parlor and bedroom, with no attempt at disguising the fact in the shape of false-faced furniture, assuming a character by day which was far from being a reality. It was a room without an atmosphere, cheerless and conventional, but two unconventional ladies now occupied it. As Paul entered the apartment one of the ladies stepped forward to greet him; her long, slender and very white hand was extended and he grasped it cordially. She was a weird sister; she was tall and willowy; a black robe, with elongated train, clung to her well-proportioned figure. Her face was ashen pale, her lips bright scarlet; her eyes jet black and sparkling; her blue-black hair fell in a profusion of unstrung ringlets about her forehead and shoulders; her voice was deep and low. With her hand, a cold one, still clasped in Paul's she turned to present him to her friend, who was half reclining in the corner of a high-backed hair-cloth sofa; but before Laurella could speak, the little lady darted out of her corner of the sofa and, in an attitude of intense curiosity, stared steadily at the youth. In her hand she held a photograph which she was comparing with his face; all this he realized in a moment and without the least embarrassment on the part of any one present: The lady spoke:—

"Yes, it is like him, very like him—and yet it is not he! Photography never catches anything but the shell; and it isn't the every-day shell, either; it is usually the stroll-after-the-Saturday-matinee shell, when one is on exhibition and self-conscious to a ludicrous degree. Turn your head a little, Paul—there, that is it," said the stranger as she compared the face and the photograph more critically, much to the amusement of the original. "Ah! that is it; if you had worn that expression when sitting for this picture it would have been infinitely better in all respects"—and she tossed the photograph from her as if it were a worthless thing.

Laurella now led Clitheroe to the sofa and presented him to the art critic; she was petite, with large calm eyes; they looked critical; and the retrousse nose was the type of a certain audacious pertness that amused when it did not startle her friends. She had the air of a professional; whenever she spoke, she seemed to be improvising light-comedy; whatever she did, she did with a dramatic air; there was nothing suggestive of the amateur; she was an artist, probably a born artist; at any rate, in one sense, the world was hers and she knew it, and was satisfied with the situation.

Paul did not catch the name; that didn't in the least matter; she knew his, and used it familiarly as if they had known one another all their lives. He seemed to fit in everywhere; he was very much at home with women, and they were with him.

Laurella had come to the metropolis on a venture. She had lectured in the mountain settlements, where she was much esteemed; had attracted the attention of a romantic poet, who offered his heart and hand at the first glimpse of her, and in due course had withdrawn both, and departed out of her sight and knowledge. Like him, she had begun to hunger and thirst for larger fame; when he won his, she resolved to follow in his footsteps—"dogging them" friends said—and was now preparing a new lecture on poets and poetry in general, and her poet and his poetry in particular. There was a prospect of a momentary sensation; the local press was assiduously working up the interest in Laurella's cause.

Now, as they were laughing together, a card, her agent's, was sent up to Laurella. The man was expecting to take the town with his sensational lecture star, and also to travel through the length and breadth of the land with her. As it chanced Paul was well acquainted with him, and almost immediately the agent suggested that Clitheroe play Cicerone to the little lady, Laurella's friend, inasmuch as business of importance was to be transacted between Laurella and himself.

Clitheroe, of course, was at their service. Willingly enough, to judge by appearances, the lady entrusted herself to his charge.

"Now where shall we go?" queried he, believing that he knew the attractions of the town. Shall it be the Marine Menagerie at the seaside? or the gardens with the retired elephant and blasé monkeys? or the cemetery?"

"Oh, none of these, Paul. I came not out for to see any of these things, nor a reed shaken in the wind; let us stroll at our own free wills; come this way."

She led him on and on, turning many corners and threading streets which he knew well enough and with which, to his surprise, she was equally familiar.

"You seem to know the town," said Paul, "have you been long with us?"

"Yes, no! I arrived two weeks ago; that is not long; but it is long enough to learn to know you all. Oh, the gardens of Hesperides!"

She paused suddenly at a fruit-stall richly fragrant, and splendid in its wealth of color. She hovered like a butterfly over the pyramids of peaches, pears, plums, apricots, the mounds of luscious grapes, the huge bunches of bananas that glowed like golden ingots; all the citrus treasures of two zones were gathered here. She engaged the amused Italian fruiterer in conversation in his own mellifluous tongue. She played her little comedy of childish delight, and played it so well that the passers-by turned at her with irrepressible smiles. The handsome rosy children in the street were detained for a moment, and saluted by her. Never before had Paul met such a woman as this. Had he been unaccustomed to the curious glances of strangers, or easily disconcerted, he would have been covered with confusion. As it was, he began to play his little part in the impromptu comedy, and to half enjoy it; and so presently they came to a modest red brick house of two stories and a basement, and he was conducted up a rather long and steep flight of steps to the front door.

The lady rang, nonchalantly, as if this were a bit of the stage business, and the comedy was proceeded with. The door was opened by a young Spanish woman, with coal-black hair that fell in waving masses almost to her feet. Her face brightened in recognition, and he wondered at finding the little lady was no stranger. Here Paul's companion had addressed her in Spanish; she had forgotten her pass-key; she was very sorry to put the Signora to such trouble. The Signora was in no wise troubled but rejoiced to see that the little lady had found a friend in the strange city. "Oh, yes, an old friend! Enter, Amigo! You are welcome to the best the house affords!"

Paul, somewhat mystified, but enjoying the situation, was invited to ascend the hall stairs and enter the front room on the right. He did so, closely followed by his companion. A very small room this; furnished with cheap furniture of a glaring saffron hue enlivened with clusters of impossible flowers and fruits of the stencil-plate variety. No attempt at decoration here; the delicate feminine touch nowhere discernible. Upon the headboard of the bed—a bed was also in the room—was pinned a sketch; it was a shaded pool, overhung by funeral boughs, the haunt of hopeless melancholy.

CHARLES WARREN STODDARD

"Now you are at home," said the little lady, waving her guest to a seat by the window and relieving him of his hat and cane; he rose to place them in the corner, but her hand stayed him.

"This house, though poor, permits not its guests to serve themselves," said she in melodious recitative. "You smoke, of course? Here are the cigarettes of my favorite brand." She offered him slender papillotes filled with fragrant Turkish tobacco; striking a taper, she lit the cigarette between his lips, took one, and seated herself upon the edge of the bed. He began to wonder who this mysterious stranger was and what she was, and why she was entertaining him in her off-hand way.

The street was a side street, and a quiet one; it could be said that it was respectable. It was not in the least fashionable, it never had been that; over the way was a Chinese laundry; next door, on one hand was a grocery at the corner; there were other residences, not to be despised, within the square. Here she seemed "at home" that is as much "at home" as she could seem anywhere; she was probably never much "at home"—she was a bird of passage.

Having finished the cigarette, the little lady tossed the wisp into the open grate, where the fire had not yet been kindled. If the two occupants of the room had not been perfectly natural people, the situation might easily have become embarrassing; as it was, they sat for some moments complacently regarding one another.

Paul was the first to break the silence.

"Do you know," said he nonchalantly, "do you know that you are an enigma?"

"Of course I know it, but every one is more or less an enigma; even to himself. Do you imagine that you know yourself?"

"Yes, I do," replied Clitheroe with some confidence. "At least I know myself better than any one else knows me!"

"That is sometimes the case," rejoined she. "I know myself thoroughly; but I also know some other people, many other people, better than they know themselves."

"Do you know me?" asked Paul earnestly.

"Perfectly; I knew you the moment I saw you; I knew you even before I saw you—the photograph told me more of you than I cared to acknowledge at first; and then Laurella and I had been discussing you pretty freely."

"But neither of you had ever seen me before," protested he, "and probably you had never heard of me."

"Oh, but I had heard of you from more sources than one; and then your eyes and your voice, and your gestures, in truth, your whole manner, enables one to classify you at sight—if one is anything of an anatomist."

"How long have you been in the Misty City?" asked Clitheroe.

"I have already told you; two weeks, no more, no less, that is two weeks more or less—a day or two more or less: I detest dates; I loathe anything that in any way limits my liberty. I want all the license one can have in life."

"You impress me as being one who has taken it—and it doesn't seem to have harmed you; I suppose you never abuse it?"

"No," after a pause, in which the mysterious stranger arose, as if slightly bored; she went to her mirror, took off her hat, and, with refreshing composure, began to rearrange her hair. Suddenly she turned; her hands were busy with the coil she was knotting at the back of her head; her elbows at that trying angle showed her charming figure to great advantage; she held a large tortoise shell pin between her teeth as she said—rather indistinctly—"I don't mind telling you who I am. We are to know each other better, and we may as well begin the acquaintance without further delay. I know you already; you cannot tell me anything of yourself of which I am not aware; you are as transparent as crystal and that is why I am going to be fond of you. But you don't know me; when we have been years together you will not yet wholly know me; you are easily attracted, easily deceived; you are ingenuous—you will never be anything else. The last comer takes you by storm, and for the time being wipes out all your past; you forget everything; you love blindly—blindly because your new love dazzles you; I say love, that is not the word to use; you think you love; you do not really love. In fact you are incapable of passion!"

Paul felt somewhat chilled; but she interested him, this woman who now had the floor, and who seemed likely to hold it as long as she saw fit. Removing the hairpin from her mouth, she seated herself in a chair, facing him, and began rocking languidly to and fro; she continued:

"As for myself—I have suffered as no one else has ever suffered; some one who was all heaven and earth to me went out of my presence as beautiful, as flawless as an angel; I shall never forget that vision of perfect human loveliness. In one hour the lifeless clay was returned to me; I never looked upon it; it was taken out of my sight; but the pool where my angel was robbed of life, of love, of radiant beauty, of everything worth living for—I sketched it; that is the finale; it hangs there over my pillow; will you see it?"

"I have seen it," replied Paul, "it caught my eye the moment I entered the room. I could not cherish such a memento!"

"Oh, no, dear child! of course *you* could not. And I'd rather not have you; you shall remain just as you are—I like you best this way."

"Then I am content to remain as I am," said he with a smile. "But you have not said where you came from, nor why you came—not that I have a right to ask."

"You have a right to ask, as you shall presently see. When I lost, in one horrible moment, all there was in life for me, I resolved to fly to the ends of the earth. I know many literary people, I have written much; it is a pleasant, though not a very profitable pastime. I made an agreement with one of the New York dailies to go round the world as its correspondent. I was still to be a free lance; my absolute liberty must never be infringed upon. I proposed to write those letters when I felt so disposed, and from whatever port I chanced to have drifted into. The remuneration I was to receive was not worth mentioning, but I don't seek remuneration; fortunately I don't stand in need of it. I came across the continent alone; I arrived in the Misty City, and took an apartment at your much vaunted largest-in-the-world hotel. For three days I was in sackcloth and ashes, despising that particular caravansary, and all who were in any wise connected with it. On the fourth day I arose, called a carriage, said to the driver: "Take me through every quiet and pretty respectable street where you are likely to see that hated signal of domestic impecuniosity—which too often is a temptation and a snare to the unwary, "Rooms to let." My final injunction was, "Don't stop until I signal you; if necessary go on forever." We started; I eyed every house on the two sides of streets that were seemingly without end. I don't like your city; it is an unhandsome city; it might have been made a paragon of beauty; nature did her utmost for it; her natural advantages are perhaps not equaled by those of any other city throughout the length and breadth of the land. But her climate is impossible; it is a cruel and beastly thing! However there is an indescribable and never-to-be-accounted-for charm in the life here which is sufficient compensation for a thousand and one defects. Realizing this, as I had from the first, I suddenly espied this little red brick house. I liked the color and the size and the shape of it; I cared nothing for its surroundings—I live within myself; I find much harmless amusement in situations and predicaments that might prove fatal to some people. I rang at the door of this house; the enchanting creature you saw below answered my ring. Her hair was cascading in torrents down her back; she was arrayed in scarlet; never was there a more delicious bit of color. She spoke to me in broken English, I answered in Spanish—we fell upon one another's necks and that settled it. I took the room and installed myself on the instant. I dismissed the carriage at the door. I sent to the hotel to have my luggage and my bill immediately forwarded; I abandoned all thoughts of touring the globe—so here I am, and here I may remain indefinitely!"

The mysterious stranger rose, adjusted her skirts, being enough like other women to find it impossible to omit this ceremony. Cigarettes were again in order, she lit one and taking it from her lips, passed it frankly to Paul. They smoked and chatted gaily upon the characteristics of the town. The place was beginning to seem cozy; Paul wondered what there was in this woman that caused him to feel so much at ease in her presence, while she was so utterly unlike other women of his acquaintance.

Presently she cried abruptly—

"Do you like letters?"

"Very much," replied Paul; he wrote scores and scores of them to all sorts of people; he was constantly receiving letters from the four quarters of the globe and in most cases these letters were quite out of the common run. Sometimes his more cautious friends had warned him against writing so many letters, and such letters as he was pretty sure to write. He had been assured that his letters, many of them were extremely compromising; that they might some day get him into trouble. To all this he paid no heed. He felt that he had already gone so far, that his only safety lay in going further. His reputation for indiscretion once well established, he believed that allowances would be made for him. If he continued to write exactly as he talked, honestly and fearlessly and without artifice or reserve, his correspondents would surely know how to take him; there was no danger of his being misunderstood in these quarters. As for such letters as were passed about as curiosities—if there were enough of these, and if they were all equally "compromising," they would cease to be novelties, and would be accepted as the only sort of letter which such a fellow as he would be likely to write. The letters he had received and carefully treasured, were, in most cases, as compromising as any he had ever written. What did it matter to him if he was misunderstood; if his letters were marveled at by some and scoffed at by others? He, himself, was quite as much the object of just or unjust censure. One thing he always strove to be, and that was, utterly honest with every one with whom he was brought in contact. Yes, he certainly liked letters, and liked to hear the reading of letters that were not addressed to him—that is, provided they were not hopelessly commonplace. They seemed to him like living pages out of human histories, and of course they were, and therefore, to him, of far more interest than any novel or romance.

The mysterious stranger, who was gradually growing less and less a stranger, seated herself upon a rug before a chest of drawers and, pulling out the lower drawer, she gathered a quantity of letters in her hands; she held them high above her head and let them fall in a scattering shower about her; she laughed merrily, like a child, exclaiming,—"Oh, how I revel in them! These are a few I carry with me; I read them from time to time; they tune me up—your true tonic must always act upon the heart. Guess whom these are from?" said she as she took a few of them and fondled them prettily in her lap.

"I'll guess they are from a sweetheart!" said Paul entering into the spirit of the hour.

"Of course they're from a sweetheart; but which sweetheart, little boy?"

As she called him "little boy" she looked archly at him, and he, half blushing stammered, "I don't know. I'll give it up."

"Did he give it up, poor child; well, he shall have his little curiosity satisfied, so he shall—they're all from my husband—my divorced husband."

"Divorced—and he still loves you?"

"Of course he does—but I'll tell you of that some other time. Now we must eat. I'm hungry. Are you hungry, boy?"

"No, not in the least. But then I'm never hungry; sometimes I feel faint, and then I know it is time to eat and I eat—if there is anything to eat."

"Poor child; was there nothing for it to eat sometimes?"

"Sometimes—in the past."

"You take life too seriously," said she with some earnestness. "You shall dine with me tonight, Paul. Come—I have a chosen seat in a chosen restaurant; your restaurants are unimpeachable, they really are, come!"

She donned her hat and a wrap, and led the way. She selected a French restaurant, famous for its cuisine; the quality of its patronage was perhaps not above reproach. She ordered dinner with the air of a connoisseur; the waiters who evidently knew her, flew at her bidding. They had not been long seated when Calvin Falsom entered and took a reserved seat at her side. Calvin Falsom, Paul's old friend, the new agent of Laurella, was poet, playwright, general utility man. Paul looked with amazement from one to the other. They took no note of his surprise. They were perfectly at ease with one another. Neither paid much attention to him; he was thankful that they did not quite ignore his presence, or find him an inconvenient addition to the party.

As early as possible he took his leave. He fancied that neither one regretted his departure, and yet the lady had been at some pains to make herself agreeable to him on the slightest possible acquaintance; as for Calvin Falsom—he had puffed Paul in the press, and shown him repeated favors and snubs. Perhaps nothing that Falsom had done, or was likely to do was much to be wondered at, but Paul, certainly, for the life of him, could not make out the present puzzling situation.

II

Little Mama

Paul Clitheroe sat nursing his soul in acceptable solitude of the Eyrie. He could have declared himself in the language of the melodramatic Moor—"not easily jealous, but being wrought, perplexed in the extreme."

He had begun to flatter himself that he knew something of the character and history of the mysterious stranger, and that perhaps she had confided to him much that die world little suspected. The confidence she reposed in him gave him an exceedingly comfortable feeling; he was ready, if necessary to champion her cause. This was his state of mind as they seated themselves in the restaurant of her choice, on the evening of the first day of their acquaintance. The entrance of Calvin Falsom upon die scene had altered the situation entirely. Once more he had resolved to foreswear the world. It was just now he was summoned to Santa Rosa to listen to the reading of Miss Juno's maiden effort. The article had been voted a success. There was much excitement among the tenants of the cottage in the Rose Garden; preparations for departure had been nearly completed; Paul had been enjoined to hold himself in readiness to set forth with his friends for Venice, at a moment's notice; meanwhile he was entrusted with a handsomely engrossed copy of Miss Juno's manuscript which he was to have published for her wherever he thought fit.

He found no difficulty in placing it; it was a clever sketch of foreign life; a sketch merely, but done with a fresh bold hand, and quite brilliant with local color. The one high-class magazine of the West at once accepted the manuscript, paid for it in advance and published it in an early issue. Nothing could be more encouraging than this. Miss Juno had planned a dinner of unusual excellence, with an accompaniment of four native wines. Paul was to be present, and the health of each was to be drunk in a separate wine. All this was to be paid for out of the price of the successful literary debut of Miss Juno. It was her idea entirely, and she took great joy in perfecting it. However, Paul pleaded some excuse, and was not present. He was forgiven, but not forgotten; he received a handsome silver pocket match-box engraved as follows: "Paul from Jack, in memory of the maiden effort."

For some weeks he had seen nothing of his friends at the Hotel de France; indeed he had not visited them since the sudden disappearance of Foxlair. When the Pompadour, in her sweet maternal way, inquired if aught had been learned concerning the welfare of the unsociable Paul, Archer had replied, "It is just possible that the boy has all along known more of the missing Foxlair than he cares to acknowledge; possibly he fears a cross examination."

"I cannot think him capable of such duplicity," said the Pompadour with gentle dignity.

"He may be guilty, nevertheless," protested Archer, and then Twitter braced up and remarked with an air of uncommon archness: "A guilty conscience smells its own breath!"

Whether Clitheroe was actually conscious that the tide of sentiment was setting against him, or whether he was for the time world-weary and in need of the repose which he found only in the seclusion of his own lodgings; or whether, still, he was more interested in his new friends than his old ones and found their society preferable, matters nothing; he did not stop to consider the case. He was rather fagged, morally and physically, and all he cared for now was to be "let alone."

There was knocking at the south entry. It found no response in the heart of the boy; he had not even the curiosity to look from the shutters and see if any recognizable forms were visible. He remained seated. The knock was redoubled, with a somewhat imperative hand. Paul, half wearied and half vexed, opened the door. There stood the Mysterious Stranger, alone. He stared in amazement.

"How long, pray, do you keep your lady friends, like the Peri, disconsolate at the gate, before condescending to admit them?" with which interrogation, delivered in her musical recitative, she brushed Clitheroe aside and swept gracefully into the room. He closed the door and followed her, in mild bewilderment. She was standing in the centre of his sitting room, turning slowly upon her heel and taking a mental inventory of every object in view.

"Will you not be seated?" asked he meekly; he felt as if he were dreaming.

"Confusion much better confounded than I ever before saw it," said the lady, paying no attention to his invitation. "All very charming; quite as I expected to find it. There is one thing missing—a mandolin; it should hang there, with that large rosary twined about it. You shall have it, it belongs here; I wonder it was not in your possession years ago. It is a marvel of beauty; a kind of music-breathing oriole's nest, all of tortoise shell and mother of pearl; so old too, a veritable antique; it bears upon its inner surface the name of the maker—Bonifazio Covilero, 1363; I purchased it in Paris at a famous sale, and paid for it more than its weight in gold. What have you here?"

She pushed open the glazed and curtained door leading into Clitheroe's chamber in the conservatory. She laughed as she glanced about her critically:

"Very pretty, very dainty,—very feminine; but I don't object to it in your case. Ah, you have one of those Madonnas I love,—but! What is this—where did you get it?"

"It is an Indian carving; it was stolen from one of the old neglected Spanish Missions down the coast. Fortunately it fell into my hands; I love it."

"Of course you do; all these fetishes appeal to the uncivilized in your nature. You are only half civilized, you know; that is why I am going to like you; I should hate you if you were like other people."

Nothing of this disconcerted Clitheroe. She might have babbled on like a brook, forever and forever, and he would have listened with pleased composure. Her flashes of analysis sometimes startled him slightly—but the sensations she awakened were all more or less agreeable.

He led the way into the larger room, and they seated themselves, facing one another.

For a few moments they sat in silence; the atmosphere was very restful; this characteristic was remarked by almost every one who visited the Eyrie for the first time.

"This is dreamland," said the lady, sinking deeper into the corner of the sleep-hollow chair—"Can you work here?"

"It is only here I work with any ease or satisfaction," replied he. "I have done so much work at that little table in the corner. It is thoroughly magnetized."

The lady turned in the deep, wide chair; she was always snuggling into corners, in search of perfect physical comfort. There was silence again; Paul hardly knew what to talk of; somehow he seemed much less acquainted with her than when first they met. She was lost in revery; he grew slightly nervous, and at last said somewhat abruptly:

"You seem to be well acquainted with Calvin Falsom."

"O, yes, we are comrades. From him I learned much concerning you before we met; he chanced to be the means of bringing us together, but his share in our destiny was the merest chance. I believe in destiny."

"So do I," rejoined Clitheroe, with an air of conviction. Then after a pause he added—"Was it your destiny to meet Falsom?"

"Without doubt," there was another pause; Paul wished the thread of conversation would not drop quite so easily. With forlorn hope he asked:

"Why do you think it was your destiny to meet Calvin Falsom?"

With a slight hesitation, as if for a moment she had considered the propriety of answering him, she said:

"Listen! I knew not one soul in this town when I settled myself in the front chamber of the little red brick house. That afternoon I called the Signora and said to her: 'Do you chance to know anyone connected with the press?' Her eyes danced as she replied 'There is a gentleman connected with the press in this very house; he occupies the small front hall bedroom, adjoining yours.' I was immensely amused. I wrote the following upon one of my cards—one announcing that I was a correspondent of the highly respectable New York daily; 'Will you kindly inform me how I can have my name placed on the free list of the local theatres?' and I requested the Signora to present the same to her hall bedroom lodger. I went forth to view the town. When I returned I found my neighbor's card lying upon my table. On it he had written, 'I have placed your name upon the free list of several of our theatres; by presenting your card at the box office you will receive the courtesies of the house.' What could be more delightful? That very evening, I sat in a solitary state at the Opera House. The play was dull beyond compare. I entertained myself with a study of the social physiognomy; there was but one face in all that audience that interested me in the slightest degree and he did interest me. I was thoroughly attracted; I don't deny that the attraction may have been almost entirely physical, but the physical element must enter into every rational condition of the human family; without it we would be as so many sticks and stones—or as the barren fig-tree of your Gospels—worthy of the scorn of Christ. After the play, I entered a car and returned to my chamber. I had retired, and was ruminating on the comedy-vein that was entering into my life—there had been such a tragedy in it of late; a dim light from a street lamp under the window shone into the room; there was a door between my room and the hall room adjoining; it had never occurred to me to examine the lock of this door: I am not one of those women who look under the bed before entering it. I heard the steps of my neighbor ascending the stairs; I heard him making his preparations for retiring. The situation was growing diverting; the movements of my neighbor began to excite my curiosity; I could interpret everything from the sound so freely communicated to me. Having arrayed himself for his slumbers, he took his pipe, lighted it and seated himself in a chair to enjoy his final smoke. He was tilting in that chair after the manner of the nonchalant and freeborn American. It so chanced that the chair was tilting toward the door that opened into my chamber; perhaps he was drowsy; at any rate he lost his balance, and fell helpless against my door; the door was not locked; its latch was not secure, it flew open; with a suppressed shriek he turned a back somersault, arriving in the centre of my apartment with neatness and dispatch. With him came a blaze of light from his room. I looked upon him with wonder, and I think I may add, delight; his face was the face I had been admiring during the evening at the play!"

"By Jove! His name?"

"His name?—Calvin Falsom!"

THERE CAME A LOUD KNOCK at the door.

"There he is!" exclaimed the little lady with unaffected satisfaction.

Clitheroe went to the hall door and opened it, expecting to find Falsom upon the steps. Instead, however, he found himself face to face with a youth of his own age—or somewhat younger than himself; a strong, beautiful face, with melodramatic eyes, such eyes as emphasize or exaggerate every passing emotion. The face was familiar, very familiar; Clitheroe recognized the graceful and spirited air of a young professional who had within a few months become a member of a famous stock company, the chief feature in the development of dramatic art in that far Western metropolis; he smiled his recognition, and invited the youth to enter. In a moment he heard an exclamation:

"O, my Roscious!"

"Little Mama" repeated he, and the two were locked in an embrace which would have done credit to any stage. As Paul entered upon the scene, and beheld the tableau of earthly felicity, the lady turned and placing the hand of the youth in that of his host, she exclaimed:

"There, you are to be brothers, and love one another with brotherly love!"

There was a hearty hand-clasp; Paul had watched the entrance of this lad upon the stage many and many a night. He had been strongly attracted by the youthful fairness of his figure; the richness of his singularly well-modulated voice; the airy elasticity of his step; the joyous and soaring freedom of his spontaneous gesticulation. He had begun to take that personal interest in the young actor which the public is apt to do, especially in the case of very young actors. Clitheroe was of course sure to make the acquaintance of the young Roscius, as he was fondly called by his sometimes effusive "Little Mama;" sooner or later he met every one worth meeting; but he didn't imagine that he and Roscius were to be brought together in so surprising a manner. They had all seated themselves, as if it were in the business of the comedy they seemed to be enacting with such relish.

"You were not looking for me when you answered my knock"—said Roscius, whose name was Grattan Field.

"No, I didn't dream of this pleasure; I thought I might find Calvin on the door step."

"Falsom will not be here," responded the lady, who was henceforth to be known as "Little Mama." "I arranged this meeting; I chose to bring you two together; my boys must always meet; and they must always let me plot for them. I saw both of you in the theatre the other night; my Roscius was not playing, but like all his fellows when he is not playing, he must be seeing others play. There was room enough at the back of the house where he was sitting; I might have sent Calvin to gather you into my fold, but I did not choose to have him in anywise associated in this first interview. I took the chance of finding you, my child, at home; had you not been at home I should have seated myself among the cypresses, in this airy Isle of Cypress, and calmly awaited the arrival of Roscius. Then together we should have picnicked in a Barmecide banquet-hall, until we had thought of something better wherewith to while away the hours. You play tonight, Roscius, do you not?"

"Yes, Mama, and it is a weary role, the lovelorn Lorenzo—I wear the costume with the alterations you suggested. Do you come to see me play?"

"Most surely; Paul will escort me there; we will await you after the play, and you, my babes, will join me at supper and see me home. By-the-bye, Paul, I've changed my address. A remittance arrived since I last saw you; a remittance always enlarges my ideas of life, and I've taken a charming apartment in the same house with Roscius. You will find your way thither tonight, and ever after bear the address in mind."

"What a winged creature you are, Madame."

"Nay, Paul, call me Mama, 'Little Mama,' if you choose; I give you leave—I command you; all my boys call me that, do they not, Roscius?"

"That they do, and when Mr. Clitheroe—"

"Call him Paul, is he not your brother?"

"When Paul hears what letters are written you by 'your boys'—well, he will be amused!"

"And now I leave you!" exclaimed the Little Mama, "I leave you two together. Follow me not—I vanish into thin air." With this she drew her skirts around her, fled from the Eyrie, and seemed literally to vanish away. Paul and Grattan were left smiling at one another in a state of pleasant perplexity.

III

A Recapitulation

Let us run over, very briefly, the affairs narrated in Books I and II.

The artistic trio, whose life among the roses pictured in Book II, came to an end with the fall of the fragrant petal, had taken flight, and Paul scarcely realized his loss. They had said to one another at intervals, "What can have become of Paul?" and then each had answered the inquiry with an apology—an apology that might resolve itself into the following: "He will come out all right in the end. He is easily attracted by a new personality; every new personality is a distraction, delightful at first, but soon, very soon, in most cases, to be outgrown. He recovers himself easily. He will probably never see Venice; at least he is not likely to see it as long as there is a brighter or more interesting face or figure dawning upon his horizon; his horizon is unhappily a very wide one; it is all embracing. Paul Clitheroe should be taken bodily out of the reach of the thousand and one influences that sway him like a weather-vane. If he were banished from Bohemia, if he were held captive in his Eyrie, and the old ruin guarded vigilantly; if he were wrecked on a desert island with his books, his memories of the past, his pen and ink and paper—with his little world of experiences to fall back on, he might do something worth while, and, to quote the blind bard, 'perhaps leave something so written to after times as they should not willingly let it die.' As it was his life was wasted and he was accomplishing nothing." So Miss Juno, Violet and Eugene departed without so much as a "good-bye" from Paul, since they could not find him at his Eyrie, or get word from him in reply to their last urgent letter.

The busy and somewhat boisterous circle at the Hotel de France made sport of him; indeed he was the legitimate prey of all the gossips, as is every one who chances to be more conspicuous than his fellows. Even the Pompadour was beginning to despair of him. She had reasoned with him often, as many another wise and good friend had, and he listening to her reasoning with the sweetest composure, was wont to upset everything with some irrelevant comment that turned the most serious argument into a farce. "Paul is incorrigible; Paul is my despair!" this was the general verdict; the verdict of men and women who were in no wise related to him, but who had involuntarily taken him into their hearts, yes, even their heart of hearts; and had likewise consciously or unconsciously, indulged his harmless whims and helped to nurse his fine or foolish fancies.

When the question arose in the editorial headquarters why Clitheroe, whose pen was well known, whose work had been a feature in the rapidly-developing literature of the West, was not regularly employed upon the columns of the daily press, the answer was, "He is of no service in a newspaper office; he has had no journalistic training; though he were to write like an angel, once consigned to the reportorial desk he would act like a fool. He can do certain kinds of writing as no one else on the Coast has done it; that is his forte; he must stick to it; other people can do other kinds of writing as well as he can."

Clitheroe knew this was the prevailing sentiment. It prevented his literary development; it limited his range; he began to feel as if he were writing himself out; as if he were repeating over and over the self-same words in the self-same way. This suspicion made it extremely difficult for him to write at all; often it was quite impossible for him to do so. The consequence was that he had the unenviable reputation of being the laziest fellow in existence; a fellow who had talents he was wasting; who had opportunities he was throwing away. He had been hailed as a poet of "great promise." Fatal prognostication! When, I pray you, does the promising poet make good his promises in the eyes of the world! A poet is not a poet till he has written his poem; when he has written his poem he is not a poet of promise but a poet of achievement!

He had, it is true, yielded to the flattery of his friends, perhaps too willingly, and at a susceptible age gathered a windfall of verses under covers and this immature volume was worked off by subscription; let it be added, in justice to the young Poet, that the mortification he endured in consequence was one of the chief causes of his foreswearing the coy muse. That experience was worth much to him; the flattery, the sometimes cruel attack, and the honest criticism he received in the columns of the local press, by word of mouth, or through the medium of the post, taught him this lesson; that the profoundest reasoners may come to most illogical conclusions; that the poorest verse will appeal to the heart of some simple admirer and the loftiest arouse the ire of a non-appreciative reader: in short, that, generally speaking, contrast the verdicts of your literary critics and criticism annuls itself. The first volume of verse had never given him one moment's pleasure; not even the sight of the printed title page, with his name in full upon it, nor the faint peculiar fragrance of the initial bound-copy as it was laid in his hands by the beaming amateur publisher. He had never cared to keep that copy within reach, nor had he thought of it a dozen times since the moment in which it made him an author.

The Pompadour wrote to him; she did not often write to him; she was a woman of rare wisdom who did not believe it wise to attempt to force him to do anything; she preferred to throw out alluring suggestions in the hope of silently influencing him; she was ever ready to sympathize and encourage; she wrote:

"When are we to see you again? The moon is waxing large and golden; these are just the nights for a drive over the winding country ways!"

Clitheroe when he read these lines thought of her with infinite tenderness. His first impulse was to go to her at once, and have a long talk with her; she was a pleasant confidante; she confided in him, as most women did. Then he opened a letter from Miss Juno; it bore a foreign post mark and had for some days been awaiting his return to the Eyrie; a bright, breezy letter. "Dear Faithless Butterfly," it began, and ended, "Your faithful comrade, Jack." She was now far away, and Paul struck his forehead with his open palm and strode up and down the room for a few moments; he began to think meanly of himself; to accuse himself of all sorts of human weaknesses and discrepancies—and then he fell to pitying himself; what could he do to be saved? He was not left alone in his Eyrie; the number of those who sought him out and led him away captive, as it were, was gradually and steadily increasing. He could not always deny them admittance; neither was it well for him to be too much alone. He needed human companionship, affection, love. He could not live long without it; if it did not voluntarily come to him—it usually did—then he must go to it, and seek it till he found it, no matter where he sought; neither was it well for it to always be companionship, friendship, love, of precisely the same kind and quality. For one day, as for one mood, one love was enough; but there came another day, and with it another mood, and then the first love was not enough; somehow it didn't fit. He believed in developing and nourishing these emotions; in order to do this successfully, a whole round of experience was necessary. The man who has had no experiences, as many have none—at least none worth mentioning—the man who has had but one experience, is certain to fall into a rut and stick there. Clitheroe had a wholesome horror of the ruts in life. He had carefully avoided them up to date; he had sometimes shot off at a tangent merely to escape from the rut which he began to feel was deepening under his feet. This was his apology for certain acts that were apparently motiveless; acts that by some were considered unmistakable evidence of the erratic. Of course it was nobody's business save his own, but this fact made not the slightest difference to those who considered his manners and customs a subject for public comment and reproach.

Sometimes, innocently enough, he became as it were a scorn and a hissing. He was not always conscious of it; he had grown somewhat accustomed to it and had become more or less indifferent in consequence.

About this time a line came from one who had, from the first, been to him as a sister; who had praised his earliest efforts in verse; who had befriended him when he was sore in need; before the public had begun to show an interest in him and to take him to task at times. She was the sweetest singer of all the tuneful choir in that young land; she was likewise the saddest singer. She wrote him now—

Dear old friend:
   "Am I never to see you again? Do you realize how long it is since you were last here? You know I cannot come to you, as others can.
   "With the love of all these years,

Ever thy devoted
ELAINE

Paul's heart quaked within him; poor Elaine, the sweetest and the saddest and the truest and the most patient and long-suffering of women and of friends; surely he was a brutish beast to have so long neglected her. So it went on from bad to worse, his gloom increasing until he began to sink under his self-reproach.

Then entered Grattan Field. Paul had seen him at the play in company with little Mama. They all supped late; had all repaired to the cozy fire-lit chamber, with its curtained alcove, where little Mama reigned like a delightful player-queen. He had tarried in merry conversation till a very late hour, and the party was finally dispersed by the somewhat unexpected entrance of Calvin Falsom who seemed sulky and ill disposed.

Little Mama had suggested that Paul spend the night with Roscius; Roscius graciously extended the hospitality of his chamber and they shared it together.

They had met repeatedly since then, but somehow the friendship did not seem to deepen or broaden; perhaps it was because Little Mama was too anxious that it should. What folly to force a friendship!

Roscius came now the bearer of gifts—a message from Little Mama, together with a package. He presented these as a prince might have presented to another prince, some royal jewel, the gift of his queen; the act was an effort worthy of his art. The truth is his art was never forgotten; it was the nature of Roscius to be dramatic; he and Little Mama played admirably together. It was as good as a play to see them as had been remarked more than once.

Paul was subject to dramatic sighing, and extravagant depths of depression, but he was more reposeful than Little Mama or Roscius and was by far the most natural of the three.

Clitheroe begged Grattan to break the seal of the package just received; they were not yet sufficiently intimate to overlook these slight formalities.

Little Mama in her prettiest chirography—it was wonderfully handsome and as easy to read as if it were copper-plate; Little Mama said:

"Jubilate! A remittance has arrived. I send you a box of Henry Clays. It is my wish that my boys smoke nothing but Henry Clays. There will be a drive this evening; meet me here,—no, dine with me, and later Laurella will join us with the most delicious bit of color imaginable. There will be a late supper by the sea—etc."

"How very droll," said Paul, opening the box of dainty cigars and offering them to Grattan.

"Thanks, I never smoke them." He grew suddenly haughty; and said to Paul: "Does she keep you in cigars?"

"These are the first she has sent me. In this note, she says it is her wish that her boys smoke nothing but Henry Clays," and he passed the note to Roscius. The scowl upon the brow of the young Thespian was admirable; from the play of his features one might have read the import of the lines; his very attitude was appropriate; clinching the paper in his fist he muttered, interrogatively:

"You will drive with her?"

"I suppose so; what else is there to be done but to accept the cigars, even if I don't smoke them myself, and to dine and to drive with her? What is this 'bit of color'?"

"'Delicious bit of color'—the fellow is pink and white with impossible hair to match; a very harmonious composition, no doubt, but with nothing whatever to back it save a due proportion of avoirdupois. He's a druggist's clerk; Mama was served by him with chocolate soda; Laurella saw him,—and—he drives with you this evening. I wish you joy of it!"

"Do you not join us?" asked Paul.

"How can I join you; I play tonight"—and O! the pride with which he stated this. "Moreover, I have not been asked to drive with you."

"Your Little Mama, no doubt, knows well enough you cannot go, since you are in the bill of the evening."

"Yes, she knows well enough!" He seated himself tragically and relapsed into moody silence.

It was all very absurd. The trivial cause, the tremendous effect, the foolish waste of emotion. Paul wondered if he ever so conducted himself, if other folks found him as amusing a study as he found the half-furious Roscius. He began to smile quietly and unconsciously. Grattan caught the smile and was offended.

"Why do you smile?" he demanded, with juvenile sternness.

"I was studying you; you are so emotional, so dramatic; I like to meet people, uncommon people; people whom I have not met before; people who are quite new to me; I like to study them!"

"Most agreeable, no doubt, to those whom you are studying?"

"Why should it be disagreeable? The fact that I find them worth studying is complimentary. Do you never study your friends?"

"I have no friends; I don't believe in friends."

"You must have been cruelly deceived, Grattan, or you would not acknowledge that."

"I have been deceived; I am always being deceived."

"Perhaps that is because you trust people whom you don't know; if you were to make a study of those you meet, you would know better whom to trust and whom to distrust."

"And if I find after a careful study of my friend that he is unworthy of me—what then?"

"Drop him. One should not be brutal or even abrupt, therefore drift away from him; neither of you need be any the worse for it."

"Paul Clitheroe!" Grattan Fields had sprung forward in his chair; his face was quite pale, his eyes were fixed angrily on Paul. "Paul Clitheroe," cried he with forced calmness. "Perhaps you will find me wanting—and will see fit to drop me?"

"Perhaps!" replied Paul in a boyish spirit of bravado; he was beginning to take an interest in the situation, and to find Grattan worth studying.

Field, paler than ever, laying his hand upon a snug package of newspapers just received by mail and not yet opened, exclaimed in a fine stage whisper:

"I've a mind to hurl this at you!" and he raised the package in his hand.

"Do so, by all means!" said Paul, who grew calmer and more amused as Grattan worked himself into a frenzy.

Whack! The package flew from the hand of the now furious youth, and struck Clitheroe full upon the cheek. He did not move; the blow stung him sharply; he was too surprised, and too confused to say anything or do anything; he sat perfectly still and looked at Grattan in dumb amazement.

It was an absurd tableau; a silly childish situation; but the wisest and best of men have some times done things quite as silly and uncalled for.

In a moment Grattan Field, flushing deep crimson to the roots of his hair, sprang towards Paul exclaiming:

"I beg your pardon; I really beg your pardon, I was only playing!"

"You never played so well in your life before!" retorted Clitheroe, with the utmost composure.

"Forgive me Paul," cried the boy, throwing himself upon Clitheroe and embracing him, "I knew not what I was doing—I was mad!"

Something in Grattan's manner; something in the warm, manly pressure of the arms that encircled Paul, something in the deep distress of his friend, won Clitheroe in a moment: All at once he began to love that wildly impulsive, strangely contradictory, utterly ungoverned and ungovernable nature.

So it came to pass that what might have been a life-long breach, proved to be the sealing of a bond of intimacy that knit them closer and closer every hour. It was agreed that upon Paul's return from his late drive—it was sure to be a very late one—he was to pass the remainder of the night with Field. Henceforth they found such pleasure in one another's society that they were seldom more than two days separated, and Little Mama, standing upon tip-toe and pointing to the stalwart young men, was wont to exclaim grandiloquently, "These are my Jewels!"

IV

The Erratic Order of Young Knighthood

They were driving in an open barouche, whirling rapidly through the sleepy suburbs of the Misty City toward the not far distant sea; Laurella with the inane "delicious bit of color" and Little Mama with Paul Clitheroe seated by her side.

The translucent atmosphere of the night brought distant objects very near to them; they seemed to be passing under the very shadow of the heights that were in reality far away; the moon glowed in the cloudless sky; the stunted oaks and dense thickets of chaparral were outlined in sharp silhouette against the stretches of smooth gray sand. The loon or the hem cried with the voice of one crying in the wilderness; on the whole it was a rather weird drive of an hour or more, which brought them to a famous hostelry perched upon a cliff, above the breakers of the Western sea.

They alighted and entered the Ladies' Reception Room; the barouche was driven away to the stable; they had come to while away some hours of moonlight beside the sea waves.

A few ennuied people were lounging upon the broad veranda, overhanging the sea; a few more were supping elegantly in the private rooms whose windows were open to the impertinent gaze of the public; still fewer were sitting apart in the larger parlor with showy, ill-used furniture, and its great mirrors festooned with fly-blown muslin. A trio of Italian troubadours of the modern school were harping and fluting to ears that paid no heed, and hearts that paid neither coin nor compliment; the one prevailing note which ran on and on without ceasing, now louder, now lower, mingling with all other sounds and harmonizing with them all, was the sob of the sea. It touched every soul that unconsciously listened to it with a kind of pleasant sadness; it hushed the riotous who moderated their mirth to listen to it; it provoked the world-weary one to turn and refill his cup of life; it struck the key-note and held it while all the elements mingled and made a more or less mournful melody. Hail, divinest melancholy!

Poor Laurella! She was reclining upon a couch where she could command the sea view; her "delicious bit of color" had quite lost his deliciousness—the color had all gone out of him in the moonlight.

Clitheroe had been beguiled into a retired corner of the hostelry. A savory supper of champagne and lobster was ordered on their arrival and they were all awaiting its announcement with some interest.

"They play well with untrained fingers, these troubadours," said Little Mama in a low voice to Paul, "but there is always a sorrowful refrain in whatever air they render."

"Why are waltzes so melancholy and so maddening?" asked he abruptly.

"Because they are so passionate. Passion is the ecstasy of love, music is the ecstasy of passion, and melancholy the ecstasy of music—these are the three in one. These wandering minstrels were born of a race that for ages lived in the land of love; they are most musical, most melancholy, because they are the incarnation of passion. Do you not love Italy?"

"Better than all the lands I know of! I am thinking of returning there once and for all, but—"

"But what?"

"But—I have not done so."

"Poor child! It was yesterday you would return to Italy forever; it is today you would dream by this semi-tropic shore; and tomorrow?"

"O, I don't know. You cannot upbraid me if I am fickle; are you steadfast in any one thing?"

"I am steadfast in love!"

"And you divorced; surely you loved your husband when you married him?"

"You silly child, I love him now."

"Then why are you not with him?"

"Did it want a weenty story told it?" She lapsed into her delightfully provoking baby-talk that made Paul feel like an amiable fool, and yet he half liked it. "Well, he should have a weenty story told in his little ear. Come!" she whispered landing him into a still more retired corner. They seated themselves in the shoulder of a lounge; the music sounded faint and far away; above all and below all, soared the sorrowful chant of the sea. She began:

"I was married when I was a child; a child in years, in body, in mind, in experience; a child! I was as innocent and as ignorant as an infant. I loved him, of course, as well as I knew how, but I was almost too young to love as a wife should love her husband. We were children, both of us; nothing better than two wilful, impulsive and unreasonable children. A

CHARLES WARREN STODDARD

babe was born to us; he was my doll, my plaything; I was exquisitely happy, and exquisitely weary at intervals. In due season another child was born. In the same moment passion crowned us both. She was the incarnation of all that a woman dreams of, longs for, aspires to. I loved my husband as I have loved my comrades many a time since. While I loved him and admired him and appreciated his various admirable and attractive qualities, I realized that we were not suited to one another. I was of a delicate physique, subject to attacks of mild hysteria, indolent, erratic, fond of my oriental ease. He was robust, sanguine, and erratic as I, a creature of a thousand changeful moods. His hours of gloom were tragical; his gaiety a kind of physical intoxication; I realized that we were utterly unsuited to one another. I told him so. I said, 'I am not the woman you stand in need of for a wife; you should be wedded to a healthful, well regulated, even-tempered woman who appreciates all your good qualities, is willing to make allowance for all your weaknesses'—he had them, as I have, and probably more of both than I—'and whose physical atmosphere is calculated to quiet you and help to regulate you; one who would never irritate you as I sometimes do.' He felt that I was right. He said to me, 'Well, choose me the woman suitable and I will marry her.' I looked about me in many quarters; I found an ideal helpmate for my husband; I invited her to my house; we were very happy together. Under my influence she developed beautifully. In the most dutiful manner my husband fell in love with her. We discussed the matter thoroughly; we analyzed her, he and I; we saw how they were admirably suited to one another; how there was but one obstacle to their immediate union, for she unaffectedly returned his love; there was no impediment save our marriage contract. We quietly journeyed to Indiana, where we were as legally separated as we had previously been legally united. We returned together, in high spirits; it was our conjugal holiday—we were equally and absolutely free. Incompatibility was the ground on which we pleaded for liberty. Now we were the best of friends, no longer incompatible; indeed we seemed never to have known each other, never to have respected and admired each other so honestly as now. They were married, they departed, and have been happy in their new life, as I have been in mine!"

Clitheroe had never known of an experience quite like this; it amused and interested him; she had confided in him; he repaid her confidence with trust, a silent bargain was compacted between these two.

"I have long believed," said Paul, with the air of a man of experience, "I have always believed that the chief reason why so many marriages are miserable failures, is because the sense of possession ruins most men."

"Yes, 'A young man married is a young man marred'—the divine bard knew what he was saying when he said that!"

"Perhaps old men are not so marrable because they are not so thoroughly marriageable. An old man is too flattered to be fretful or exacting, when he finds any one kind enough to put up with him. He is in his dotage, of course, and dotes on her; she therefore can fool him to the top of his bent," said Paul.

"The more fool he!"

"Why not the more fool she—unless her chief motive in such a marriage is to take the upper hand and keep it? I have a friend," continued Clitheroe, "a wonderfully fascinating woman who was adored by a man she had been the making of. He was intellectual, refined, extremely clever; one of the most brilliant conversationalists I ever listened to. He idolized the woman who stood between him and the world; he valued her as he valued no one else on earth. They were always together. It became a matter of conjecture what relation they bore to one another. One day she said to me, 'I am about to make a concession to the laws of conventionality—he and I shall marry.' I, boy though I was, was emboldened to say to her, 'You are about to make the mistake of your life; just so long as he is not quite sure of you; just so long as you may at any moment go your way, and bid him go his, and refuse him admission to your presence, he is your slave. Just so soon as he begins to realize that you are his, that you are his property, at his command, to go where he says go, to stay when he says stay—you are his slave, and you will lose his love—perhaps his respect also.'"

"Well, she denied it and thought you a fool," said Little Mama.

"Yes, she denied it and married him, and in six months I lived to hear her acknowledge that I was right in every particular. Do you think I was right?"

"Yes and no!" replied Little Mama. "Had your friend been any other sort of a woman, she might have retained the love of her lover, even though he became her husband. I grant you it is a severe test; the marriage state. I ought to know something of it."

"You evidently do," rejoined Clitheroe, feeling that there was perfect safety in making such a statement. "As for myself—poor me—I have always felt that to marry very early, while love is still an all-absorbing, rhapsodical state, and to lose one's wife in a little season, after having a beautifully rounded experience, in which there was no shadow of weariness or distrust; to live on cherishing this sacred and enrapturing memory—Oh! that has seemed to me the perfect state!"

"You are an idealist, my child; you will outgrow all this. What a contradiction you are, Paul! Just now you were preaching the dangers of the married state to a lady of far more experience than you, no doubt, for you know you don't know much of the world; and yet you long to be a widower."

"Yes, a widower—but no husband. I must be free. Would you marry again?"

"Marry again! I am of a long-lived family; I shall very likely live to be a hundred. I married at sixteen, I shall probably continue to marry every ten years so long as I live."

"You married at sixteen, you are past twenty-six—you have told me that already; are you married now?"

"If I am married now, what earthly difference could it make to you?"

"Could you be here, as we are here tonight—without him?"

"Without whom?" Little Mama looked sharply out of the corner of her eyes at Clitheroe.

He replied, "O, I don't know, exactly, Calvin Falsom, perhaps."

Enter waiter announcing supper.

"Come child, I am famished; give me your arm," and Little Mama piloted Paul to the small supper room, where Laurella and the pink-and-white-one with all his color heightened in the glaring light, were awaiting them.

A conventional quartet is pretty sure to embrace only general themes; one cannot become truly confidential unless one has the good half of a duet to himself. Supper ended, the couples paired again and went upon the sea-side gallery to watch the moon as it slowly descended toward the horizon. The night was far spent when they returned to the city. Laurella said adieu at the door of her lodgings, the same where he had met her, and Little Mama, so short a time before; yet how long ago it seemed to him. Then the barouche wheeled away to the house where Little Mama held sway, where Roscius was no doubt deep sunk in slumber and where Paul was to seek repose.

After Laurella and her friend had left the remaining two occupants of the carriage to themselves, Little Mama turning to Clitheroe said:

"You have not heard of the Order of Young Knighthood, unless Roscius has told you of it?"

"He has told me nothing of it. The Order of Young Knighthood?"

"Yes, there is an Order of Young Knighthood. The rule of the Order is known to the foundress, the Lady Superior alone. Only the elect are admitted to its privileges. Its novitiate is a secret test of all the manly virtues. Every Knight of this Order is a Knight by right divine, for he has been tried as by fire and found not wanting; he has been tempted in divers ways; if he passes through all these perils unscathed, he is admitted to the mysteries of the Order, and great is the joy thereof."

She was waxing eloquent; Clitheroe listened attentively; he wondered what she would say next; she said: "Ever since I have known you, ever since the first moment I laid eyes upon you, there in Laurella's room, you have been blindly passing through a novitiate; you have unconsciously been proving yourself worthy to be called a knight. It is *my* Order of Young Knighthood; *I* am the founder, and the superior and all the various officers in one. With *me* rests all power, and the only power. *I* admit the successful candidate to full communion after he has survived the ordeal of the novitiate."

"But may he not know that he is a postulant? Is it fair, is it just to him to be leading him into temptation and throwing stumbling blocks in his way, and he ignorant of the traps laid for him, and even of your motive in laying them?"

"It is the only fairness, it is the only justice. Were he conscious of his novitiate he would be always on his guard. He would not be his real self. I would perhaps never know his true character. I must know him, know him thoroughly, as I know every Knight of the Order. I must lead him into temptation as often as it is necessary to prove his power of resistance; thus only may I hope to deliver him from evil when the evil day dawns on him; for there are those it were vain to deliver from evil since they are in themselves evil to the core. Thus only may I learn to know him as I have learned to know child Roscius, as I have learned to know you, Paul."

The barouche drew up at the door of her lodgings: Paul assisted her in alighting; with her latchkey he admitted her to the house, and preceded her up the long flight of stairs that led to the landing at her door. He was about to say "good night" and thank her for the uncommon pleasure she had afforded him; a light was burning dimly in the room at the far end of the hall, occupied by Roscius; Paul was upon

CHARLES WARREN STODDARD

the point of turning toward it when the two hands of Little Mama were laid gently upon his shoulders, and they stood face to face. She lifted her face to his; it was pretty and pale; it showed lines of weariness, world-weariness, showed them very faintly. When the burden of the day began to grow uncomfortable, Little Mama cast it off and fled she cared not whither. Neither would she borrow trouble, though she were in sore need and it was the only thing she could borrow. The one rule of the Order of Young Knighthood which she dwelt upon night and day was this—"Cast your cares upon the careful and you shall be cared for in due course."

"Paul," said she, "you have been tried and found not wanting; you have been tested, and nobly have you stood the test. Would you like to enter the noble Order of Young Knighthood?"

He started in delight.

"Then," said she with the air of a vestal virgin: "You may kiss me—just once—right there!"

V

Our Lady of Pain

Clitheroe had been thinking of Elaine and accusing himself in a helpless, hopeless sort of way, of having been cruelly neglectful of her. She had begged to see him; had asked him to come, as of yore, to the quiet little house where she lived in nun-like seclusion.

He had sent word that he was coming; he had meant, from day to day, almost from hour to hour, to visit her, to talk over all the past with her, to advise with her, and, if possible, to come to some definite conclusion concerning his future plans.

"I will go today," said he, in a noble determination to shake himself free from the temptations and snares that of late had increased mightily, and were hedging him about on every side. I will also write to Jack and tell *her* that I'm coming; I'll get ready and start at once; somehow I don't seem to be quite myself of late; he said all this in an audible aside. He had been thinking of Jack, in the dear old way, and calling himself a fool for having let slip the opportunity of crossing the sea with that artistic trio, even though his financial prospects were not very encouraging and he might find himself cramped when he got abroad. Still, this would be no worse than if he were to stay where he was, doing little or nothing, for there was little or nothing for him to do. He must be doing something, and that right soon for his over-indulgent landlady was beginning to show signs of impatience; so was the laundress; so also the long-suffering Treasurer of the Club. Moreover, his wardrobe needed replenishing; he was conscious of betraying visible and undisguisable evidences of wear and tear from head to foot. He would write to "Jack," and as soon as he had written to "Jack" he would go to see Elaine, and tell her all about it; and then he would somehow, *somehow* settle up with the world, and depart in peace.

This was one of the delightful resolutions so easily made, so much more easily unmade than kept—many of them indeed impossible to keep—and more's the pity. Coming home from a late breakfast, one morning, he had settled the whole thing in his mind; he had never before settled it quite so satisfactorily to himself and all parties concerned. Unlocking his door and entering his sitting room in the spirit of a new man, what was his surprise to find Little Mama quietly seated in his deep sleepy-hollow chair, patiently awaiting his arrival. She had been admitted by his landlady, who found it quite impossible to resist her blandishments and who certainly had more fear of the stranger's displeasure than of Clitheroe's surprise.

"And has my child been feeding on the fat of the land, that he has kept his Little Mama waiting the whole morning?" she asked soothingly.

"Alas, no," replied he, slightly disconcerted. "It was the dread of having to select the least distasteful dish of a score of distasteful dishes, that compelled me to walk the streets for some time before the ordeal, and to sit longer than I cared to, over my meagre breakfast."

He threw himself into the long East Indian chair and stretching himself full length, looked inquiringly at the ceiling.

"I've a great and glorious plan," said Little Mama; "you shall hunger and thirst no more forever. My infant, my infants all, shall be lapped in luxury; we will lead the ideal life—we will sorrow no more, and like the Lotus Eater, forget the past."

"Ah, me!" sighed Paul who dared not venture a reply.

"I have it all here, in this little book—O, the richness of it! Come, all ye that labor and are heavy-laden; without money and without price, come! Come!"

"Come where?" asked the boy a little pettishly; he was hungry, though he had breakfasted.

"I have a noble scheme. I will establish a temple for the honor and the glory of Young Knighthood. I have selected the site of this temple, and the temple itself is already habitable. There is a wooded valley opening upon the sea; a river flows through it; upon the bank of the river is a roomy manor house, rude certainly, such a house as woodsmen love to dwell in, but that house is ours for a song—for a song my child, do you hear me? and who is there of us but can sing and sing right merrily?"

"Ah, Little Mama! It's all a dream," moaned Paul, with a sigh; "Songs cannot butter my bread for me; I cannot sing right merrily with my rent unpaid. Truly!—truly!" cried he with a strange earnestness in his voice, a thing which his listener had not noted before—"Truly I'm getting a little weary of dreaming and singing for suppers that don't begin to satisfy me!"

"Paul!" cried the imperturbable, "listen to my scheme. I have property in the East—property which I cannot enjoy myself, and will therefore dispose of, that others may enjoy it. With the moneys thus obtained, I will open my lordly castle by the sea. I will see that the table, though it be a rustic one, is laden with such viands as befit the palates of Young Knighthood. Only the Elect shall be admitted to that board, and their lives under my lordly, if lowly, roof, shall be beautiful and Knightly. I will, myself provide such means as are necessary to the establishing of the ideal life and then my boy, then my fairest Knight shall be the chosen one."

Clitheroe was silent for a moment; the Little Lady had risen and was pacing the chamber with a graceful swaying motion; her hands were folded behind her; her face was lifted; she seemed to be walking in a dream. He regarded her curiously, and asked in a doubtful voice—

"Will Roscius be there?"

"Of course he will be there, as often as he can make his escape from the Theatre; sometimes he does not play for several nights; the bill is changed frequently in this hurly burly town!"

"Will Laurella be there?" he continued.

"Laurella will be there whenever the spirit moves her. She is to lecture and may be often far from there!"

"Will the 'delicious bit of color be there?'"

"A delicious bit of color was never known to worry anybody or anything. The art decorative must not be forgotten or ignored even when we are in the midst of the beauties of nature. Do you object to the 'bit of color?'"

"No, certainly not; I don't see much of Knighthood in him. If we were thrown together night and day for days and weeks and months, he could never be anything to me more than what he now is, a kind of animated dummy; he reminds me of the lay-figures that come to life and caper all about the stage; one is amused at the spectacle; one is relieved when, at the close of the pantomime, they return to their proper places."

"Listen to me," said she, earnestly.

"There is a blessed relief in variety, in change of any kind. Were it not that the world is made up of all sorts and conditions of men, the world would be simply intolerable."

"O, yes, everyone knows that! Will Calvin Falsom be there?"

"Probably Calvin will be there at intervals. This Bower of Beauty, though its atmosphere is that of extreme remoteness and seclusion, lies close at hand. In one hour by ferry and mountain train one comes to the edge of Avalon—it is the valley of Avalon. There one descends, and winding through the wood, rounds a handsome hillock and finds one's self in the enchanted vale. It will be easy for Calvin, for Roscius, for even you, if you find yourself ill at ease or restless, to come and go at your own sweet wills. Those who choose may contribute according to their means, and pleasure to the general fund. It will be liberty hall; it will be as far as we are able to make it so, the higher life, the life where temperaments are the first consideration, and affinities the next, and where conventionalities are throttled at the threshold. Do you not like the picture?" She approached Clitheroe; her eyes were sparkling; this was the very life, the thought of which would have once enchanted him; in those days, at the first suggestion of it, he would have thrown all else to the winds; he would have followed her blindly, have trusted all to her with the trustfulness of a child; like a child he would have danced in delight at the thought of so romantic a situation; it would have charmed him even as a fairy tale charms; but now, somehow and for some reason not quite clear to himself, he hesitated; he showed no enthusiasm in the venture; he betrayed little curiosity. Suddenly the lady who had been regarding him steadily for some moments, shrugged her shoulders, turned upon her heel and went toward the door; with quite another air, and a voice that had an artificial ring in it she said, almost gaily:

"French this afternoon at the usual hour. My cherubs must not neglect their accomplishments, though the heavens fall. Dinner when the lessons are well-said, and some manner of pastime afterwards. My child finds the world growing wearisome. He needs change; we will plan it all tonight. Adieu!" and with a pretty flutter of her small hand she disappeared. Clitheroe had not risen; he was evidently forgetting his manners, or himself.

No sooner had the abrupt departure of Little Mama left him time to gather his somewhat scattered faculties than Clitheroe put the room in order, locked the windows, seized his coat and cane, and departed with the key of the outer door in his pocket.

He crossed the beautiful bay, sparkling in the brilliant sunshine and fretted here and there by the scudding flocks of wild duck; he touched on the shores of Arcadia and grew happier in a moment. "I know where the trouble lies," said he to himself—yet a passerby might have overheard him, he was so in earnest,—"I am too much in the world; I see too many people, hear too many noises—the clash and the clang of traffic; my eyes are blurred, my ears are deafened; my heart is sick of it all. I must get out of this; by Jove, I must make my escape in one way or another." In this mood he came to the door of the modest cottage, sitting back from a quiet street, in the midst of a well kept garden filled with old fashioned flowers. A large Maltese cat purring upon the door mat, arched her back at his welcome, approached and threw her sleek body against his trouser's leg in ecstatic abandonment. He took the beautiful creature in his arms for a moment, listening to its loud yet muffled purring, and was as happy and contented as that incarnation of contentment in his arms. While the two were gradually magnetizing one another, the door swung open and there stood a sad-faced, slender woman of pronounced Spanish type, with eyes that were full of tenderness and regret.

"Elaine!" exclaimed he, entering the cottage with puss still in his arms.

"Well, dear Paul," said she, in a low voice, a contralto voice in the minor key, "I began to think you were never coming again!"

"Of course I was coming some day, any day. Every day I was on the point of coming, but little things upset me so easily."

"Little things upset most of us, dear Paul; the wonder is why the great things don't seem to accomplish more destruction. One is less startled at a great and fearful crash, than at a little noise that signifies nothing. It is the little annoyances that worry one's life out."

"Then what am I to do—seek greater annoyances?"

"No, I wouldn't do that; they will come to you if you will only have patience. I'd try to avoid the occasion of lesser annoyances."

"How avoid them?"

"I would keep them to myself for one thing; I would come to see Elaine oftener for another thing—I don't annoy you do I, Paul dear?" and she smiled her weary smile.

"No, you don't," cried he, dropping the cat and throwing his arm about the waist of his friend as he led her to the lounge in the corner. It was a pretty room; the souvenirs of artist friends hung upon the walls; an old-fashioned set of bookshelves on one side of the room was stuffed full of books—most of these the gifts of their authors; the grate, wherein no fire was laid, was a pretty study of still life—like a grotto in some nook of the sea. A very sweet, but a sad place, alas! Paul never visited there but he felt the sorrow of Elaine weighing upon his heart when he went out from her. Her life had been one long and bitter disappointment. Her poems had won the praises of the noblest poets in the land, but they had not sold as they should have sold, far and wide, and to the world in general; even to the well informed literary portion of it, her name was too little known. Losing one after another of all who were nearest and dearest to her, she was by force of destiny compelled to lead the life of a slave, in order to clothe and feed herself though modestly enough. From morning till late in the evening she was on duty in a public office; only on Sundays and national holidays could she call her soul her own. This was Elaine, the sweetest singer of all the tribe in that golden land of song—and the saddest by right of silent, prolonged, helpless and hopeless suffering.

"I don't know what is to become of me, Elaine," said Paul, as he sat by this self-elected sister, with his hand about her shoulder and her head resting upon his breast. "Something will have to be done pretty soon. I shall be at bay before long."

"The weakest show fight when they are at bay; perhaps you will surprise the kind friends who give you credit for but few of the manly virtues."

"Perhaps," said he dubiously; he continued after a pause, and with much deliberation: "Sometimes I think that the best thing I can do is to retire from the field."

"And acknowledge yourself beaten?"

"I need acknowledge nothing; I owe no acknowledgment to any one."

"You owe it to your friends," interpolated Elaine with some spirit— "You owe it to your friends to achieve something in life. You are not striving to. You are wasting time, opportunity, youth, health, energy, everything. Why do you not go to work at something and stick to it until you have achieved the end in view?"

"And, if you please," asked Paul, with a slight touch of irritation in his tone, "at what shall I go to work?"

"O, something, anything! Only don't lie idle—and don't be led away by your too flattering and seductive friends."

"Something, anything," murmured he with the faintest shadow of sarcasm traceable in his voice.

"Yes, dear Paul. Why do you not write? You have talent; there are those who have claimed for you even genius; you have reputation; not one on the Coast has a better local fame; you have only to write—"

"Only to write?" broke in Paul impatiently. "I have been writing almost ever since I could push a pen, and I've never been able to make a tolerable living by it. I am not paid for my work as other people are paid for theirs; often I am not paid at all—and this I suffer at the hands of people, editors, who are supposed to be honorable men. I find myself writing upon certain themes until I begin to repeat myself and am woefully conscious of the fact. I branch out into a new field, and begin to write with hopeful enthusiasm. What is the natural consequence? My articles are rejected; or cut all out of shape and misprinted; I know I write a bad hand; it all ends by my, very likely, getting no pay for my work. This is very inspiring, isn't it?" and he patted Elaine on the shoulder as if to encourage her not to be too sorry for him, and to assure that he would stand by her even if she had to weep over his total collapse.

"It is not very encouraging, dear Paul; we neither of us have much to thank this great and glorious country for." After a pause, "But you can do something else? You are not like us wretched women—'the world is all before you where to choose.'"

"Yes, and I may choose and choose again and again, until I begin to realize that the only thing left for me to do is to get the world all behind me."

Elaine laughed a hollow sort of laugh; she had considered the world and her battle with it from every point of view; often she had weighed the pros and cons in the balance and wondered whether it were worth while to battle longer.

"Paul dear," said Elaine with a sigh, "why don't you go on the stage? You have voice, manner, perhaps as much talent as the majority—and there is a new experience for you."

"I don't care for the stage; I found private theatricals very jolly, especially the rehearsals, which were great fun. We all believed ourselves to be artists; we felt as artistic and as conspicuous and superior as possible. I outgrew that stage of development pretty soon; hang it! I outgrow everything too soon; nothing lasts—nothing! nothing!"

"Friendship lasts at least with you, and no one has less reason to complain on this score than you have; if it doesn't, Paul, it is probably your own fault," said Elaine.

"I hate private theatricals now," continued Paul. "I go and go and go again to the play; I sit through it because I'm not obliged to listen to it; the play plays on whether I'm interested or not; the public is paying attention and roaring with laughter or wiping its eyes, but it's nothing much to me. I don't wish to go on the stage, yet I don't know where else to go; I want to rid myself of the necessity of catering, or trying to cater to the whims of the Editorial chair."

"Have you talked with Harry English on the subject?"

"I've talked with all sorts of people as plainly and as plaintively as I could, or dared to talk. One doesn't quite like to go up to a fellow who is perhaps envying one and has a fine opinion of one and cry out to him, 'I say old chap, I'm starving, can't you lend me a dollar? I haven't eaten a crumb since I dined sumptuously with the Pompouses last night and I can't eat anything until this evening when I am invited to dine with the Upstarts, unless some one will pay the price of a mug of beer and let me nibble at the free lunch counter.' This isn't a very pleasant state of affairs. Come now, is it Elaine?"

"Of course it isn't dear boy; speak to Harry English; see if there is no practical suggestion that he can make. Won't you promise me to do that?"

"O, yes, I'll do it, but nothing will come of it, you can bet on that."

Elaine brought cake and wine. It was very pleasant in the little cottage. Paul told, with many amusing embellishments, his adventures with his friends the Samaritans and Philistines; Foxlair and Little Mama were duly discussed; the story of Miss Juno attracted Elaine; she would gladly have met such a person had it been possible; but Elaine saw few, very few people, and these were friends of years agone. She was our Lady of Pain, born to sorrow and to suffering, and bearing her heavy burden without bitterness or complaint.

Paul was returning to the Misty City that night; the late boat was crossing the still water by moonlight, and as he sat on the breezy forward deck watching the city they were approaching—a picturesque outline of shining hills pricked with a myriad of lamps, like clouds of fire-flies floating in the west—he was startled by a large soft hand being placed gently upon his shoulder, and a familiar voice calling him fondly by name.

"O, Harry, I'm so glad to see you!" exclaimed Paul as he threw his arms about the portly figure of Harry English; "This is so awfully fortunate, our meeting just now. I've been all the afternoon with Elaine, having such a talk. She's been scolding me again."

"Has she, poor dear girl! Well no one has a better right; she's been a mighty steadfast friend to you, my boy."

"I know she has; I know it well enough; but now she wants me to go on the stage; what do you think of the idea?" It was thus Paul began his brief if not brilliant dramatic career as recounted in Book I.

"She wants you to go on the stage, does she? Well," he paused and added, "Paul, I have never advised any one to go on the stage; I never will do so; but if the time should arrive when you want to go on the stage, come to me and we will talk about it. But you are not to stop writing?"

"I can't afford to write," replied Clitheroe: "If I had money, if I had an independent income, just enough to keep me in food and clothes, and find me a shelter from the weather, I'd rather write than do anything else in the world. I'd like to write for all my extras; I think I'd enjoy them more if I worked for them. But I mustn't be worried; I must be independent or I can do nothing."

"Poor child, you'll find it hard lines on the stage, I fear."

"Of course I shall; but it is hard lines everywhere with me, when it comes to the question of earning bread and butter. All I want to know is that every month I am to get so much money, every week, I mean,—that sounds better—and that it will be money enough to cover my expenses; they are not very great, you know!"

"Well, my boy," said Harry English after some moments of meditation, "you might make twenty dollars a week to begin with!"

"That is more than I did Europe on, Harry; it was mighty close sailing most of the time, but the memory of it all is most delightful."

"Of course it is, of course it is," said Harry English in a kind of refrain that had a good deal of tenderness and consolation in it.

The boat drew near the slip where the red and green lights threw glaring reflections upon the inky waves. "Well, Paul," said Harry English taking the arm of the boy, as they walked up the dock toward the caravan of street cars where they were to separate, "think it over well; look about you; see if there is nothing else to be found for you to do; if not, and you resolve to try the stage, then come to me. Mind you, I don't advise. Anything else, almost anything else were better; so enquire among your friends; why I should think any one would be proud to help you, my boy!"

"Yes," cried Clitheroe as they parted in the crowded street, "yes—they are so damned proud to do it, that nothing ever comes of it!"

VI

A Contradiction

Had the inner life of Paul Clitheroe been made known to the public, no one would have been more surprised than his most intimate friends. He was certainly misunderstood; he was a contradiction, as we all are, and in his case especially, the two sides of his nature were as unlike as possible. It is said of many weak characters, such a one is his own worst enemy; this was distinctly true of Clitheroe. He seemed to enjoy depreciating himself; he may have been perfectly honest in the valuation of his literary talents; he had ceased to compound verses, because the verses he had compounded no longer seemed to him worth compounding. He was painfully conscious of his inability to battle successfully with a world with which he was not in sympathy, and in which he took little or no interest. He knew he could not give satisfaction to his employers as porter, salesman, or accountant; perhaps even as silent partner he would be found of no avail. He had, when quite a youth, chosen to enter business rather than continue his studies under tutors whom he never loved; but usually feared; no text book had any attraction for him. With a willing spirit and a ready hand, he had modestly awaited an opening in which he hoped to gain an honorable livelihood. To be sure, his business career had been anything but a brilliant one. "A shirker of responsibility; one willing to live upon his friends"—alas, this was the unenviable reputation he had innocently and unconsciously achieved.

He had a glib tongue, when it was set wagging. He could say more in a minute than he could stand to in an hour; he had a lively imagination that was apt to run away with him. He had much sentiment; a love of the fine arts; his temperament was hyper poetic; he had also a lively sense of the ludicrous, often through the fear of appearing silly or soft in the estimation of those he loved and respected, he would, in the midst of some lofty flight, cut a metaphorical pigeon-wing that turned everything into ridicule. Therefore he was thought frivolous, flighty, even foolish at times; yet it was his supersensitiveness and a kind of feminine shyness, born of delicate pride, that caused him to misrepresent himself. He used to boast, in his boyish way, of his indifference to this, that or the other, when at the moment he was suffering because he could not be quite indifferent. He delighted to think himself a savage; to declaim against the demoralizing influences of civilization; he yearned to overthrow conventionality with a brave sweep of the hand, and yet he was the final result of a long system of over-education, over-refinement, and over-religious zeal.

He was frothy; he delighted in boiling over at intervals to the amusement or the scandal of his too indulgent friends.

All this time, while he was seemingly flitting from flower to flower, Clitheroe had paid frequent visits to a venerable Jesuit who had been the dearest and the best and the wisest of fathers to the boy. No one man knows another man so well as a confessor his penitent. Often Paul had flown to his Ghostly Father in a kind of desperation which nerved him to re-enter the conflict with a brave heart. More than once, when the worst had come to the worst, he had received that practical aid which enabled him to tide over a financial crisis that promised to sweep all before it. He was always certain of gaining moral strength and encouragement, and he left his venerable friend with a light heart and a more hopeful spirit.

One evening Paul strolled into the theatre; he was trying to accustom himself to the idea of an intimate and personal association with plays and players. The play-house was never distasteful to him but he was not in the least stage-struck and all the glamour of the foot-lights had vanished from before his eyes.

He had not been long seated in the house when Calvin Falsom joined him. Calvin was the bearer of a message from Little Mama. "Would Paul not join her in her loge?" Of course he did so. Grattan Field was there; Paul was presented to a group of youths, possible candidates for the Noble Order of Young Knighthood; none of these interested him much; once they might have done so, but he seemed to be undergoing a serious change, and he was beginning to realize it. He had not seen his Little Mama for some days; he had not attended the French class which she gratuitously called together and instructed when so disposed; he had sent neither explanation nor apology for his seeming neglect of one who was more or less devoted to him; yet she was as bright and airy as ever, and with her uncommon tact she made no reference to the silent interval during which she had more than once questioned, both privately and publicly, the motives of Clitheroe's unaccustomed reserve.

During the *entre act* the occupants of the loge, all save Paul and Little Mama, withdrew and she turned to him with the query:

"What have you been doing of late? Do you join us in the Forest of Arden?"

The double barreled question did not startle him. He knew something of the sort would be put to him at the earliest opportunity. He withstood the simultaneous discharge with becoming composure and replied:

"I have been meditating many things, chief of which is how to make a livelihood. I am beginning to grow weary of Bohemianizing. Probably I shall not be able to join you in the Forest of Arden."

"Is he growing weary of Bohemia? Evidently the time is out of joint. He should consult his physician. Probably he needs dieting."

"Possibly, Littlest of Mamas; we all stand in need of it now and again; it is no doubt an excellent corrective, as well for the body as the soul!" Paul's eyes were wandering listlessly about the house.

"And the soul likewise? Was his spirit vexed? What troubles him now? I suppose some new goddess has shattered him for the time. What a child he is, a mere mite of a child, with little pains and pins to fill him with infantile agony. It is all very funny, when we stand apart and see ourselves as others see us; you know there are times when we *can* do that, if we only have the knack of it, and the knack of it is infinitely better than powder or pill."

"I am not hungering for powder or pill!" rejoined Clitheroe with the slightest possible tinge of resentment in his manner of speech.

"When one stands most in need of a corrective, one is apt to be the least conscious of it. With whom have you been to catch this ill-fitting melancholy?"

"With no one in particular."

"With every one in general. That is unwholesome; one of your temperament should be exclusive; many natures feed upon you and leave you utterly exhausted; you, on the other hand, could never gain anything from them."

"I know that well enough; it seems to me I must have always known that, but I cannot keep aloof from people as long as they will not suffer me to abide in peace." Then after a pause, "I begin to realize that the only way for me to get on in the world, is to get out of it."

"You issue your Bull with papal facility, my child; you may get out of the world, but it will be a weary day for you until you get back again."

"I'd like to try it," muttered Clitheroe, heaving one of the semi-tragic sighs for which he was noted.

"Let us not dramatize any longer," cried Little Mama, impatiently; "Honestly, and without more ado, what are your plans?"

"I shall throw aside my pen, since it does not bring me enough to pay for my bread; I may go on the stage, though God knows I'd rather not."

"On the stage?"—she looked curiously amused. Clitheroe continued:

"I can go, whenever I am so disposed. Harry English will engage me at a moment's notice. I shall know in a week whether this is to be my fate. Meanwhile I must put my house in order—that is break up the Eyrie—for in any case I am likely to be starved out of it."

"I have a plan better than the one you propose"—said Little Mama, after thinking earnestly for a few moments: "I have a plan, the dramatization of a charming story. There is a young priest in it, an enchanting fellow, the very role for you. There is one character which I always intended to play myself, a part in which I can wear the divinest wig, a wig I purchased in Paris, and which I wore for a whole season when I was the companion of Schneider, and appeared in Opera Bouffe with her company, just for the fun of the thing. I could not sing, but as we were touring the provinces, I was confident and looked well in the eyes of the ever sympathetic villagers. There is a part I can work over so as to fit Roscius like a glove. We will choose three or four others of our coterie, all sympathetic; Calvin shall be our agent, and I shall be manager, and we all shall be stars; we shall start right here, and make enough out of our opening to set us on our way; we shall be one happy family of wandering Thespians; we shall require little scenery, and be able to play anywhere on the slightest provocation. We'll become famous, under names that shall ring as music in the ears of the great public; we shall make the triumphant tour of the world!"

Paul smiled; once, and not very long before he would have danced with joy at so delightful a prospect; it would have seemed possible then, yes even plausible, and his dreams would have been of triumph after triumph in every clime; one long enrapturing round of profitable pleasure, with never a shadow to fall across his path. Now he only smiled; smiled a little sadly, perhaps, as if he were conscious of having lost interest in something that would once have given him joy; as if he were outgrowing himself and beginning to look with disapproval on the dreams and schemes that were once his delight.

VII

A Passion Torn to Tatters

They had talked on till the fall of the curtain, Little Mama and Clitheroe; the house was rapidly being deserted. "Come," said she, "Roscius is longing to see you; you have not been as brotherly of late as I would have you. Come, we will have oysters in my room, and champagne; your blue devils must be exorcised!" She took his arm and he was conducted, not unwillingly perhaps, to her apartments. It was chill and the place was in much disorder; he kindled a fire in the grate; she gathered her garments together and bestowed them carelessly in a corner. From various nooks and lockers were abstracted viands: the good red wine of the country was not lacking; a small table was soon laid: Little Mama having retired to the curtained alcove, arrayed herself in a becoming tea-gown.

"Roscius is late tonight," said she, as she made her appearance in fascinating dishabille.

"He has been much in the bill of late," replied Clitheroe, wishing to say something, and not knowing just what to say.

"Yes, he has had many parts to study, but he likes study; his heart is in his work and he is steadily developing; have you a good study, Paul."

"I really don't know; it is long since I learned a part; when I was learning it took my time, for there was time and to spare; amateurs are not usually pressed for time."

"Well," said Little Mama consolingly, "the Pendragon Dramatic Club will have little studying to do after the repertoire has once been mastered, and it will not be extensive. Better do a few things well, than many indifferently, say I; moreover, we shall not tarry long in a town, for we have the whole world before us. You know one can play in English all through the Orient, and skirt Africa and Oceanica, into the bargain. What richness! You, my child, shall write the most bewitching book of travel."

"And adventure?" queried Clitheroe, growing interested.

"And adventure, without doubt! O, there will be numerous 'hair-breadth' escapes by flood and field, page after page of them, world without end—amen!" and Little Mama struck a charming attitude under the flaring chandelier. She was Thespis, seeking more worlds to conquer.

Enter Grattan Field, his eyes snapping, his teeth gnawing his nether lip.

"And what has happened to the child?" asked Little Mama cheerily; she always viewed dramatic situations from a comedy standpoint.

"What has happened?" muttered Field in fine scorn of the lady's cheerful mood. "Everything has happened. I shall quit the company, I shall quit the town, I shall quit the State. What a loathsome people—a generation of vipers; out upon them!" and with an appropriate attitude and his eyes flashing fire, he banished the children of men from his sight. It was quite an exquisite touch of art. No one present save himself knew the occasion of his rage; no one cared much to know it, that was always the last thing to be considered; the rage, the picturesque rage was all sufficient, and this had come to be one of the chief and most entertaining features at the impromptu *conversazione* where Little Mama so joyfully presided. She never lost her composure; though the vail of the temple were rent in twain, she was *debonnaire* to a degree.

Something had offended Grattan Field; it may have been a fancied slight on the part of an innocent person in the audience; it may have been a misunderstanding with a fellow professional, or an unpleasant encounter in the street, on the way home, or only a wish to work himself up into a fury in which he apparently took mental and physical delight. He was hysterical, as many men are; he could become half-delirious by an earnest effort of the will. When his end was accomplished, whatever that end may have been, he was very apt to dissolve in tears and become quite lamb-like in his extremity.

Tonight he was bent on making a scene; some one was to be sacrificed, it mattered little who; his best friend was as likely to fall a victim to his rage as his worst enemy. It were vain for him to pour the vials of his wrath upon the devoted head of Little Mama; she would have accepted his libation as an unctuous ointment, and most likely have criticised very cleverly his speech, gesture, attitude, from the dais of her artistic standpoint. He knew this, and spared her to spare himself. Seeing pen, ink and paper upon a table in the corner, he seated himself in desperation, with just a touch of the serio-comic in it, and began to write. Clitheroe, who had become accustomed to these bursts of passion, began pacing up and down the room in a fit of abstraction. The great, the momentous question of the future was again beginning to oppress him; his spirits were low; presently Little Mama summoned her boys to supper. Grattan was absorbed in his letter-writing; Paul had at that moment reached the little table where the actor was writing: Paul heard the call to supper and paused mechanically; his mind was really very far away. He was not conscious of his position in the room, his eyes were fixed on vacancy, he saw nothing; but he seemed to be seeing the sheet that Grattan had covered with writing and suddenly the writer paused, turned abruptly, sprang from his chair, pushed Paul roughly from him, and cried, "You were reading what I have written!" he then seized the letter, tore it in fragments and dashed them into the grate.

His fury was sublime; he was unquestionably foreordained to the stage; all the dramatic instincts were born in him; he could not help dramatizing every situation, and here was a capital opportunity, silly enough in itself, certainly, but capable of being worked up into something noisy if not effective.

Clitheroe was staggered; nothing had been farther from his thoughts than to glance at the writing of his friend; he had never dreamed of doing such a thing; it would have been morally and physically impossible for him to have done it.

"You saw what I was writing," Grattan repeated furiously. "How dare you look over my shoulder?"

His manner, tone, insinuation, were insulting. Clitheroe grew pale, and began to tremble, as he always did when laboring under suppressed excitement.

"I did not see what you were writing; I was not even conscious of being near you at the moment!" he replied, with what calmness he was able to command.

"You would steal upon me!" continued Grattan in his fine frenzy,—"you would see if I had a secret from you!" and with a wild gesture of contempt he seized the hall door, threw it open and turned furiously upon Paul: "Blackguard!" he hissed between his teeth, as he disappeared beyond the door that was slammed after him.

Little Mama was in gales of laughter: this was more delightful than French comedy; she applauded, she shrieked with joy at what she considered such admirable evidence of the true dramatic ability in both her boys, two future members of the Pendragonions. She now had hopes that Paul would develop great talent in the line of subdued intensity: she was charmed, she was jubilant.

"Now Paul, child, that was beautifully done; go at once to your knightly brother, and kiss and make up."

"Pardon me, Little Mama," said he, with a tremor in his voice which was several tones lower than its usual pitch; "I don't care to see him again." He seated himself upon the hearth rug and looked steadily into the burning grate; he was silent; she continued:

"You act like two infants. You should both be punished and put to bed. You know well enough Paul, how flighty Roscius is; how at times he must tear his passion to tatters or his passion will explode him. He is probably at this moment bathing his pillow with tears, and upon your entrance will fall upon your neck in paroxysms of repentance. Come now go to him at once; tell him I bade you go."

"No, if you please!" replied Paul heaving a deep sigh, "I have thought it all over. I find it is impossible for me to respect any one who is capable of believing me a sneak, or an eavesdropper, or a spy, or anything unworthy. Whoever does so falls farther in my estimation than he is capable of debasing me in his. If he were to return this moment and assure me that he meant not a word he said, I could not love him as I have loved him for I know that he harbors mean suspicions. How otherwise could he imagine me so low as to take advantage of him in any way? What cared I for his writing? How could it possibly have concerned me—unless he had chosen to inform me of it?"

"You are taking this quite too seriously, Paul; such things are done continually, and done by very good and clever people; you cannot deny that in your church, your schools, your domestic discipline, there is a system of espionage that is quite as ignoble as eavesdropping, or the spying out of private correspondence."

"I am saying nothing in the way of a denial; all I say is that whenever and wherever I discover that this degrading system is in vogue, there and then I sever all connection with the parties concerned, whoever they may be. Therefore"—he clutched his breast with his two hands and struggled for a moment as if he would wrench something from it, and this invisible something he cast into the flames, exclaiming,—"there, out of my heart I tear my love for Roscius, and cast it root and branch into the flames!"

"How intense you are," said Little Mama lightly, and yet not without a shade of weariness in her air: "Come, let us sup!"

"No, dear Little Mama! I have no stomach for anything tonight. Let me go back to my Eyrie. That is where I belong. I should not have left there; I should have kept more to myself. O, I wonder if I shall ever be able to do that? Good night, dear. You have been very good to me and I thank you for it, but I must go now; I am getting tired of all this!"

"Stay Paul," said she, catching him by the arm as he turned to go; "I will call Roscius; he shall not treat you so, under my roof. He is brutal, and shall acknowledge it before us both!"

"Do not go to him!"—it was Paul's turn to detain her; "I am gone, good night!" and he passed hastily onto the stair-way where he met Calvin Falsom ascending.

"Ah, good evening, Clitheroe! How is your Little Mama? Falsom's voice and manner were equally exasperating.

"Good night," cried Paul from the foot of the stairs, and the next moment he was striding through the lonely streets to his lonely home on the hill-top.

VIII

In Eclipse

S ome weeks passed and all this time—it seemed a long time to Clitheroe—he had known nothing concerning Grattan Field, heard nothing from him, seen nothing of him; in one sense only had he seen his former chum; he had watched him enter upon the stage on two or three occasions, with the foot-lights between them, and the memory of their friendship began to seem like some play upon which the green curtain had naturally fallen. Roscius, his face, his form, his voice, all were familiar enough, but they seemed far off, and as if Paul had no more interest in them than had any one else in the audience! Well, he had not; their intimacy was a thing of the past. Had there been the slightest effort on the part of Grattan Field toward a reconciliation, Paul would not have hesitated to take his friend by the hand once more, and to do his best to feel and act towards him as they had felt and acted when they were almost all in all to one another. But his love for Grattan had died and made no sign, and Paul had flung from him the corpse of it.

Clitheroe really wished to see his Little Mama; he had expected to see her at the Eyrie, but she kept aloof—just why, Paul could not conjecture. He resolved to visit her; he would have done so before, but he feared he might encounter Roscius which, to say the least, would have been embarrassing to both parties. So he had remained away; moreover he had been too busy to write to her, though under other circumstances it would have been quite like him to write a letter daily.

At last, he resolved to brave the situation and call upon Little Mama. The house, as he entered it, didn't seem quite familiar; this supersensitiveness is often an inconvenience; the man who is susceptible to surrounding influences—atmospheric, climatic, physical, mental, moral and religious, may know the highest happiness, but the penalty he pays is to know also the profoundest misery.

There was something wrong in the house of Little Mama; there was something missing. Clitheroe, who had found the street door unlatched, ascended to the room wherein he and Roscius had, when last they met, enacted their silly melodrama in one act, one scene. There was the door of Roscius' room; on the glazed transom over it Paul saw what he thought to be the shadow of his quondam friend. Yes it was a shadow—a moving shadow, and he tapped lightly at Little Mama's chamber door; no answer. He tapped again; still no answer; he tried the door, it was fastened—she was out, or not visible. He descended the long stairway, feeling somewhat like a sneak. On the pavement, just as he emerged, he met Calvin Falsom. Calvin chaffed him professionally about his "conversion" to the stage. Calvin always treated Paul as if he were a spoiled child, and had many a time made light of him in print. Calvin asked, with a drawl:

"And wherever is your Little Mama?"

"I don't know" replied Clitheroe. "I've just been to her door, and it is fast; I got no answer to my knock."

"Is it fast? Why she must be away; perhaps she is out of town? Would you like to say anything to her? Possibly I could find out where she is."

"I'd like to see her very much," said Clitheroe innocently enough—he was innocent in many respects; he had never questioned the propriety of the late visits Calvin Falsom was wont to pay to Little Mama, because he could and would have done the same thing himself without a thought of impropriety—and in reality without giving any cause for scandal among honest people who might have been conversant with the state of affairs. Falsom annoyed him often; he thought the playwright presuming, and wondered that Little Mama could allow so much familiarity on the part of a man who surely was not one of her "boys."

"Where *is* Little Mama?" asked Clitheroe.

"O, I don't know exactly; I'll try to find out for you. Meanwhile if you wish to send her word, I'll volunteer to do my best to forward it to her. In this way I may be able to get an answer for you."

"I wonder where she is?" said Paul, as if musing and in reality being much perplexed—"Are you sure she has left the city?"

"Let us see!" Falsom lead the way into the house and to the door of her chamber; taking a key from his pocket he unlocked the door, and opened it without hesitation. "Walk in," said he, somewhat to the surprise of Paul, who was growing more mystified every moment.

There was not a trace of the lady left in the apartment. The wardrobe doors stood wide open; there was nothing hanging within save a garment or two, evidently the property of Calvin Falsom. Paul looked about in mild dismay. He thought of the scene Roscius and himself had enacted when last they met, and now—

"Where is she?" he cried anxiously.

Falsom took him by the arm, and gently but firmly led the way out into the street. Once there, he said,—"Your Little Mama has flown!"

IX

The Transit of Little Mama

Throughout the fretful season that followed, Paul had found some distraction in his speculations concerning Little Mama. She seemed to grow more and more a mystery from day to day. Her disappearance was still unaccounted for. Calvin Falsom, the celestial messenger, passed between them, bearing glad or sad tidings to and fro. Sometimes Paul ventured to question Falsom concerning the friend whom he really missed, and often wanted to see, but no satisfactory explanation was ever rendered by the man who evidently knew most concerning the situation. Clitheroe in his letters had sought to win from the lady permission to visit her. He met one friend who confessed to having seen her, but when and where and how, remained as great a secret as ever. The Fates conspired against him, and in despair, he finally abandoned all hope of ever again meeting her in the flesh.

Letters came to him; they were written in an undiscovered country, from whose bourne Calvin Falsom returned at intervals; these letters were addressed from the "Mountains of the Moon," "The Valley of Delights," "Avalon," "So Near and Yet so Far;" there was no post-mark, there was no clue, by which Paul might search out the hiding place of the mysterious Little Mama. Sometimes a shower of fragrant petals fell from the envelope as he opened it; or he would find tiny, exquisitely tinted feathers pricked through the margin of a letter and so he would assure himself that his Little Mama was in pastoral seclusion, and that it was as vain for him to seek her as to seek a star in space.

It is needless to say that this correspondence was merely an aggravation; very delightful in its way, to be sure, but still an aggravation. Paul at last lost patience. He wrote to Little Mama a pathetic letter; he told her, in so many words, that he was weary of waiting for a fortunate turn in his affairs; that he wished above all things to see her; that if he were permitted he would gladly fly to her—no matter where she might be hidden; that life was fast becoming unendurable; that things could not go on as they had been going of late—from bad to worse; and he had therefore concluded that he should "his quietus make" with anything he could lay his hands on.

Would this melt the adamantine heart of the Littlest of Mamas? Apparently it would not.

One day Falsom, whom Clitheroe was growing to scorn, met that young man, and in his rather overbearing manner, said to him, "I shall have something to show you presently; suppose you join me at the library on Thursday next—say, about three o'clock?" Clitheroe explained to Falsom how impossible it was for him to get away from the office of the "Saturday Matinee," where he had been pot-boiling of late. "Not that the rush of business is likely to prevent, but who will inform the anxious enquirers that 'the editor is not in'?—he cannot always do it himself—you know"—said Paul.

"Do you call yourself a citizen of the Land of the Free, and don't dare to meet a friend for a few moments during business hours?"

Falsom was a Britisher to the marrow of his bones, and he delighted to chaff the boastful American.

"I call myself nothing," replied Clitheroe, testily; "least of all a citizen; I have never voted, and I shall never vote!"

"I am the last man in the world, Paul, who is likely to force you to do your duty towards your government; but I must confess I cannot see why you should not be permitted to take half an hour off in a life time—I am not likely to make any future appointments with you. Come now, say that you will meet me at the library on Thursday—do you promise?"

"Yes," said Paul, doggedly, wondering why Falsom should be so anxious to make an appointment with him.

Of course it was supposed to be something the playwright had written, yet it was not often that he honored Paul by requesting an opinion concerning his literary work.

At three precisely—it must be remembered that he was now a business man and had acquired business habits, Paul was at the library. He strolled through the various rooms discovering no signs of Falsom and was about retreating hastily, rather glad to make his escape, when the librarian, who was an old friend of Paul's, beckoned him. Now the young man was certain to be kept in conversation for a time; meanwhile Falsom might make his appearance; Paul felt that there was no escape for him. The librarian led him on and on; Paul talked freely and ingenuously, as was his nature. It mattered nothing to him that ladies and youths and book-worms and school-girls came to the desk where he was standing, to examine the latest additions to the library; none of those attracted his special notice; if they stared at him he was quite used to it—more so than ever, since his experience on the stage.

One listener was persistent; a lady in the deepest mourning; the heavy crape veil that fell from her forehead to her feet, made it impossible for any one to distinguish her features. She was intent upon the titles of the latest fiction, ranged in a long row in front of the librarian's desk; she seemed, in a sense, unconscious of his presence, for she brushed against him without apology; and as he moved to allow her to continue her research, she still lingered. When the librarian's attention was demanded for a few moments and Paul withdrew to one of the alcoves—he felt quite like lingering now, the atmosphere of books was always grateful to him—he turned to find the crape-swarthed embodiment of modern grief within arms' reach of him. He was somewhat startled, but at that moment he caught sight of Falsom, and went towards him. As they were in conversation the lady in crape passed him, and for a moment he felt her hands upon his arm; as she reached the door she turned her glance full upon him; without raising her veil, she bowed profoundly, turned and disappeared.

Clitheroe looked enquiringly at Falsom. "Do you know her?" asked he.

"Not I; who could be expected to know any one in mask and domino?—that's what her grief aspires to."

"Well; tell me why you asked me to meet you here today? I was on hand at three, sharp; and have been waiting all this time."

"I must apologize; what I was hoping to show you is not presentable. We will meet later, and talk it over." Falsom seemed in haste, and departed abruptly.

As Paul was about to follow in deep perplexity, the librarian called him and said, with an amused expression, "Some one, an entire stranger to me has asked me to place this in your hand."

Paul took it mechanically; it was a letter addressed to him in a strange hand. He did not pause to open it; without delay he returned to the office of the "Saturday Matinee" and found, to his relief, that the editor had not been within sight of the place during his absence. Suddenly he remembered that the letter in his pocket was still unread. He broke the seal; 'twas from his Little Mama: she, it was, who had donned widow's weeds and brushed against him in the library; she had longed to see him, but could not, and would not ask him to her hiding-place and, fearing to disclose her identity in public, she lingered by him for a few moments unrecognized, and with a silent farewell withdrew.

So she had been, from the first hour of their acquaintance secretly married to Falsom! Her retirement was necessary; her wee child, the child of Falsom, was now absorbing her whole mind, and her whole heart and her whole soul. Therefore she disbands the noble, if erratic, Order of Young Knighthood, and commends her well-beloved knights to the tender mercies of the One who, in His beneficence, and tender mercy, drew them to her when she was well-nigh distracted, and when their society and their love were her consolation. Paul, dazed, feeling as if he had played the fool as no one had ever played it before, passed a sleepless night. He avoided the club; he feared to lay eyes on the "perfidious" Calvin Falsom. He resolved never to again trust any one—save the one faithful Elaine.

X

In the Valley of the Shadow

C alvin Falsom having given hostages to fortune—two of them, one of each sex—one summer's day drank off a sleeping potion; he had long been ailing, and his intense physical sufferings, having become unbearable, he gave up the ghost in premeditated haste.

If any one had ever doubted the moral courage of Little Mama, they could no longer question it in this shocking crisis. Her philosophy such as it was, was sufficient unto the day. The body, having been handsomely encased, was borne by his Bohemian brethren to a public hall in the Misty City, and placed upon a dais. While a favorite Glee Club sang sweetly of the inevitable, the apparently unavoidable happiness into which the departed soul had somewhat abruptly, to be sure, entered, two mourning women, swathed in black, entered and seated themselves at the head of the casket. They passed, unescorted, through the length of the hall where all Bohemia was assembled, and had seated themselves in marble calm—black marble calm, facing the assemblage, but with their heavy crape veils falling to their feet, a little murmur of surprise swept through the house: it seems that the world, even the small gossiping Bohemian world, knew not that Calvin Falsom was a married man, and the father of two children. It remained for them to conjecture that one of these mourners was his widow, the other her bosom friend who shared with her grief; they were in very truth Little Mama and Laurella.

The slight sensation caused by the apparition of the veiled ladies having subsided, the Glee Club once more lifted its choir of voices in inspiring strains. Then Harry English rose, and with the right royal spirit of good fellowship which had won him the hearty affection of all with whom he had been brought in contact, pronounced an eulogy on the virtues of the once sprightly Calvin Falsom. It would seem that man's chief end was to be as much like Calvin Falsom as possible; that for such as these the kingdom of heaven was ever at hand. Indeed, no one who was present and who was hale and hearty, could help congratulating himself that his prospects in the life to come were so brilliant and so sure. Then the choir sang a song of rest—a very sweet and soothing refrain.

At this stage of the rather original services, there was a pause. No one seemed to know exactly what was to follow, but, when the silence was becoming embarrassing, Little Mama arose, and stood at the head of the coffin as cold and stately as a statue. With appalling deliberation, she turned her veil back from her face; the face was as pale as the face in the coffin over which she stood. Placing her hand upon the casket to steady herself, she spoke with icy calmness, in a voice so well-modulated its slightest whisper was audible in the farthest corner of the hall. A deathlike stillness possessed the assembled multitude; the situation was almost melo-dramatic, and thrilling to a degree. She spoke of his many manly virtues, and extolled the human qualities which made him a helper of the weak and frail, because he himself was weak and frail. "Why should he hope to be, or strive to be, any better than another?" cried she, in a clear penetrating voice as mellow as a flute; "Was not Christ, that exquisite creation, the ideal hero of history, tempted alike as we are, in all things? and there are millions who claim for Him the title of the very Son of God!"

"My husband," she called him repeatedly as she prolonged her address, for she was now bound to claim a father for her children; her children were not present, but she had published to his friends and to the world that Calvin Falsom had left a widow and a family; who could gainsay it? She sank into her seat with a creditable show of emotion. The friends of the deceased, who were present in great numbers, seemed struck dumb with amazement. Not that any relationship he might have borne during his life to any one was calculated to astonish them much; but that his marriage could have been kept so long a secret even from his intimates, was, to say the least, startling.

Laurella arose when the widow had veiled her face; they were both tearless, these extraordinary women; Laurella bore public testimony to the truth that had fallen from the lips of the bereft. She was a living witness to the contract which had legitimatized the children of her friend, and the open confession of those mourners must forever set at rest the tongue of gossip.

The choir now sang a parting song, full of tenderness and trustfulness and hope. No prayer was offered; perhaps no one who knew how to word a presentable prayer in public, was present. The casket was conveyed to the hearse; the funeral cortege, preceded by a conspicuous band, departed for the cemetery, and the journals of the day contained interesting and attractive accounts of the Bohemian Obsequies.

CHARLES WARREN STODDARD

A few days after the grave had closed over the mortal remains of Calvin Falsom, his widow, with her children, returned to her old home in the Eastern States to wear out her widow-hood. She had stated it was her intention to marry once in ten years, and her third husband has left her free to fulfil her plans. Laurella, having sought in vain to achieve success on the lecture platform, fell into a decline, withdrew to seek the shelter offered by the widow of Calvin Falsom and duly paid the debt of nature, after having borne patiently sickness and sorrow and famine. In her last hours, she wrote to the husband from whom she had been long separated, and he graciously visited her, bearing floral tributes to her bed of death. It was her last request that he write her brief memorial and give it to the world, and this he did, with a grace that touched the hearts of his readers.

XI

The Beginning of the End

It began to seem as if the end could not be far away. It was written in the stars that his hour should come and he began to feel that it was drawing very near: He seemed to have heard the ominous *click* that in old fashioned clocks gives warning that the gong is about to strike the hour—this was what he had been waiting for these many months past. All he needed now was a climax to complete his round of experiences in the Misty City. This climax he proposed to precipitate alone and in secret.

He carefully packed all his earthly possessions and stored them in a bonded warehouse. His landlady knew nothing of his plans, though she lent a willing hand in the dismantling of the rooms Paul had so long occupied; a willing hand because it was a kindly hand; as for herself—she would gladly have continued to trust her old tenant for room-rent on to the day of doom, feeling that sooner or later the money would be forthcoming; she liked to have him and his friends under her roof, she had grown so used to them.

So Paul suddenly disappeared.

Miss Juno was sure she had discovered him under the cowl of the Franciscan Friar at San Francisco del Deserto; she was perfectly satisfied on this point. What more natural than for Paul to become a lay-brother in a romantic monastery on a holy island in the Venetian Lagoon? That was quite in his line, the costume and the customs that prevail at such an unworldly retreat. He had sought the rest he had been in search of nearly all his life and probably had found it. So Miss Juno wrote at once to a friend in the Misty City and gave the glad tidings an impetus that carried them far and wide.

Though it is the easiest thing in the world to mistake one person for another,—it is done daily and a thousand times a day—nobody for a moment questioned the fact of Paul's having joined the Franciscans at San Francisco del Deserto, as stated by Miss Juno in her letter. Of course he had turned Friar; it was the most natural thing in the world for him to do. There the matter was dropped and Paul became a memory that faded day by day until his name was scarcely ever mentioned.

CHARLES WARREN STODDARD

Now, what really happened was this. Having packed everything he valued and seen it safely stored, he settled with his landlady and went down to the Club. It was his P. P. C., though no one there suspected it, and with just a touch of sentiment—he walked through the rooms alone; he saw at a glance that the usual habitues of the place were employing themselves in the same old way. Though he had not been there often of late, no one seemed much surprised to see him; he passed through the suite of rooms without addressing himself to any one in particular; a glance of recognition here and there; a smile, a slight nod, now and again, this was all. Having made the rounds he returned to the cloak-room, took his hat and cane and departed.

From that hour dated his disappearance. From that hour the Eyrie saw him no more forever.

XII

By the World Forgot

For a long while he had been listening to the moan of the sea—the wail and the warning that rise from every reef in that wild waste of waters. There was no moon, but the large stars cast each a wake upon the wave, and the distant surf-lines were faintly illuminated by a phosphorescent glow.

There were reefs on every hand, and treacherous currents that would have imperilled the ribs of any craft depending on the winds alone for its salvation; but the *"Waring,"* its pulse of steam throbbing with a slow measured beat, picked its way in the glimmering night with a confidence that made light of dangers past, present, and to come.

It had struck eight-bells forward; midnight; the air was warm, moist, caressing; it stole forth from invisible but not far distant vales ladened with the unmistakable odor of the land—a fragrance that was at times faint enough, but at other times was almost overwhelming; from the heart of the tropics only, is such perfume distilled; few who inhale it for the first time can resist its subtle charm; its influence once yielded to, the soul is soon enslaved and the dreams that follow are never to be forgotten.

Eight-bells, and silence broken only by the swish of the propeller as it ploughed slowly, deliberately, through the sea; the slap of the ripples under the prow, and an occasional harp-like sigh of the zephyr in the softly-vibrating shrouds; Paul Clitheroe had stolen out of the cabin and was sitting by the companion-way on the port side. A small ladder still hung there, for there had been boating and bathing just before dinner, and there was sure to be more or less fishing whenever the weather was favorable. Moreover, it must be acknowledged that the yacht was liberty-hall afloat, yes, adrift, on a go-as-you-please cruise, and things were not always in ship-shape.

An old half-breed Trader, who knew these seas as the star-gazer knows the skies, was in the wheelhouse; every wakeful eye among officers and crew, was at the prow peering into the depth in search of danger-signals; every ear was listening intently for an order from the lips of the pilot, and for the first whisper of the wave upon the reef.

Meanwhile the vessel crept forward with utmost caution, barely ruffling the water under her keel.

One Bell! Two Bells! Clitheroe had for a long time been sitting unobserved by the companion-way. He had dined with a riotous company and withdrew as soon after dinner as possible; this privilege was freely accorded him, for he was at intervals gloomy, or silent, and his companions were quite willing to dispense with his society. Hilarity had ceased for the night, the fact was patent. The truth is, there was apt to be something too much of it aboard that ship. When a young gentleman, on the death of a distant relative, comes suddenly into an almost fabulous fortune, he is apt to set about doing that which pleases him best; in all probability he overdoes it. If he be fond of any society and is willing to pay for the purchase of it, he will find no difficulty in supplying himself, even to the verge of satiety.

A certain gentleman who shall be nameless in these pages but who came to be known among his followers as *The Commodore,* finding himself heir to a fortune, chartered a yacht for a summer cruise, and invited his friends to join him. The yacht had been for some weeks the scene of unceasing festivity; the joyous party on board her had passed from island to island, the feted guests of Kings and Queens and dusky Chiefs; feasting, dancing, and the exchange of gifts—these were the order of entertainment night and day.

It was a novel life for most who were on board, filled with adventure and spectacular surprises. The Commodore's hospitality was boundless; the appetites of his guests insatiable. But Clitheroe had seen all this from quite another point of view; he had been a native among the natives; admitted into brotherhood with the tribe he had lived the life they lead until it had become as natural to him as if he had been born to it. Their thoughts were his thoughts, their tongue, his tongue. He was thinking of this as he sat by the companion-way, in the silence, unobserved.

Three Bells! He rose and going to the open transom, looked down into the cabin. The long dinner table had been relieved of dessert-dishes, but the after dinner bottles were there in profusion, and cigar-boxes and cigarettes within convenient reach; it was an odd scene; a picture of confusion in a dead calm. The lights were burning low and there was no sound save the hoarse breathing of some of the revellers who had subsided into uncomfortable positions and were too heavy with sleep to seek easier ones. Clitheroe saw at the head of the table the

Commodore, stretched back in his easy chair; he was fast asleep; there was no doubt about that. His guests one and all were dozing. The drowsy stupor that follows a debauch pervaded the whole company. I venture the assurance that not one person present could have been aroused in season to save himself or herself had the ship at that moment struck a reef, and foundered.

There they were, dimly outlined under the cabin lamps, the companions with whom for a season Clitheroe had been more or less intimately associated in the Misty City; the Bohemians who had found it an easy and pleasant thing to flock upon the deck of the *"Waring,"* one foggy afternoon, and set sail on a summer cruise. The Commodore invited them for his entertainment, and because he was a mighty good fellow and could afford to. They went for a change of air and scene, in search of adventure—and moreover they were sure of luxurious hospitality for at least six months. Clitheroe joined the company, not only for the reason that there seemed nothing else for him to do, but he was glad of the opportunity of revisiting a quarter of the globe so very dear to him. This voyage, he thought, might re-awaken his interest in life; at any rate, he could lose nothing by taking it, and that settled the question for him.

The singers, the dancers, the painters and poets made life very lively in that summer sea; it was a case of sweet idleness with wine, women and wits, and all the world before them where to choose. It must be confessed that Clitheroe had enjoyed himself in the society of these old comrades—you would recognize most of them were he to name them; but tonight, or rather this early morning he had begun to moralize, as he peered down the transom upon the half-shadowy forms of those feasters who had fallen by the way. He was asking himself if it paid— this high-pressure happiness that knew no respite save temporary insensibility? He began to think that it did not, and with a shrug of his shoulders and a faint sigh, he turned away. He was about to resume his solitary watch, for he could not sleep on such a night, when his eye was attracted by a flitting shadow weaving to and fro astern; it seemed to be soaring upon the face of the waters; was it some broad-winged sea-bird following in their wake ? He watched it as it drew near, growing larger and larger every moment. No! it was not a bird; but it was the next thing to one.

Out of the darkness was evolved the slender hull of a canoe, the wide, many ribbed sail, and the dusky forms of three naked islanders.

CHARLES WARREN STODDARD

They had not yet taken note of him; with a sudden impulse, he stole up to the transom, and standing over it so that the lights from the cabin-lamps shone full upon him, he waved a signal to the savages enjoining silence, and bidding them approach with caution.

In a few moments they had wafted themselves noiselessly up under the companion ladder, and there, with suppressed excitement, he was recognized. Old friends these, pals in the past, young chiefs from an island he had loved and mourned.

There was a moment of passionate greeting, and but a moment, in the silence under the stars, then, with a sudden resolve, and with never a glance backward, Clitheroe, descending the ladder, entered the canoe and it swung off into the night.

Two hours later, the *"Waring,"* having run clear of the labyrinthine reefs, steamed up and was out of sight before daybreak.

"AND WHAT IS LEFT? DUST and Ash and a Tale—or not even a Tale!
MARCUS AURELIUS

A Note About the Author

Charles Warren Stoddard (1843–1909) was an American novelist and travel writer. Born in Rochester, New York, he was raised in a prominent family in New York City. In 1855, he moved with his parents to San Francisco, where Stoddard began writing poems. He found publication in *The Golden Era* in 1862, embarking on a long career as a professional writer. Two years later, he traveled to the South Sea Islands for the first time. While there, he befriended Father Damien, now a Catholic saint, and wrote his *South-Sea Idylls*, which were praised by literary critic William Dean Howells. After converting to Catholicism in 1867, he began his career as a travel writer for the *San Francisco Chronicle*, journeying to Europe, Egypt, and Palestine over the next five years. In 1885, he took a position as the chair of the University of Notre Dame's English department, but was forced to resign when officials learned of his homosexuality. Throughout his career, Stoddard praised the openness of Polynesian societies to homosexual relationships and corresponded with such pioneering gay authors as Herman Melville and Walt Whitman. Primarily a poet and journalist, Stoddard's lone novel, *For the Pleasure of His Company: An Affair of the Misty City* (1903) is considered a semi-autobiographical account of his life as a young writer in San Francisco. Among his lovers was the young Japanese poet Yone Noguchi, who moved to San Francisco in his youth and became a protégé of Stoddard and the poet Joaquin Miller. Recognized today as a pioneering member of the LGBTQ community, Stoddard is an important figure of nineteenth century American literature whose work is due for reassessment from scholars and readers alike.

A Note from the Publisher

Spanning many genres, from non-fiction essays to literature classics to children's books and lyric poetry, Mint Edition books showcase the master works of our time in a modern new package. The text is freshly typeset, is clean and easy to read, and features a new note about the author in each volume. Many books also include exclusive new introductory material. Every book boasts a striking new cover, which makes it as appropriate for collecting as it is for gift giving. Mint Edition books are only printed when a reader orders them, so natural resources are not wasted. We're proud that our books are never manufactured in excess and exist only in the exact quantity they need to be read and enjoyed.

bookfinity™

Discover more of your favorite classics with Bookfinity™.

- Track your reading with custom book lists.
- Get great book recommendations for your personalized Reader Type.
- Add reviews for your favorite books.
- AND MUCH MORE!

Visit **bookfinity.com** and take the fun Reader Type quiz to get started.

Enjoy our classic and modern companion pairings!

Classic & Modern

9 781513 295374